SHE GOT ANOTHER MAN AROUND MY KIDS

ZARKIA

She Got Another Man Around My Kids

Copyright © 2024 by Zarkia

All rights reserved.

Published in the United States of America.

Published by Cole Hart Signature, LLC.

Mailing List

To stay up to date on new releases, plus get information on contests, sneak peeks, and more,

Go To The Website Below...

www.colehartsignature.com

CHAPTER ONE
KAILA MOFFETT

"I don't need you standing over me while I do my job, Caroline. I'm sure you have a lot of paperwork to do, so why don't you focus on that?"

Caroline was pushing sixty years old and always in my fucking business. She was one of those older black women who took charge of our coworkers and me just to run her swollen ankles up the stairs to snitch. I'd worked as an administrative assistant for a nonprofit organization for the past eleven months, and outside of dealing with her daily bullshit, it was easy work. Filing papers, making copies, setting up meetings, and all the other shit that came with the job made the $3,000 bi-weekly paychecks worth it.

"Remember last time you didn't copy me on the email regarding the budget for the school supply drive. I want to be included in every communication you send moving forward. This is not up for debate. And if you have a problem with it, we can go upstairs and talk to the CEO about it," Caroline badgered, using her finger to poke the back of my seat as she spoke.

Shaking my head, I returned to my computer to finish the email I'd drafted. With spring break approaching in a few weeks, I knew I would take off that week and needed to be ahead with my workload. I despised coming back with work piled on my desk, especially since Caroline's helicopter ass was clocking my every move.

"Kaila, I'm so sorry to bother you. The police are at the front desk looking for you. I believe it's regarding your children." The front desk receptionist, Henry, approached, keeping his voice at a whisper so my coworkers in the cubicles surrounding me couldn't hear.

"The police?" I mouthed.

My racing heart and quick-moving feet had me heading to the reception area before I could process what he'd told me. Rounding the corner, my daughter Taika tried to run toward me, but an officer stepped in front of her, blocking her access to me.

"What is going on? Why are you stopping my child from coming to me?" My voice echoed through the lobby.

"Ma'am, is there a private area we can speak in? There was an incident with your children."

"Where's their dad? What happened?" I quipped.

Henry cleared his throat before suggesting we step into one of the smaller conference rooms just off the lobby area. I walked in first with one of the police officers trailing me. Looking back, I expected my children to be behind us, but they remained in the lobby.

"Please tell me what's going on. I don't like my children being stopped from approaching me. I didn't do anything to them, and I know they didn't do anything to anybody. So, Officer..." My eyes quickly scanned her uniform for her name tag. "Luma, what happened?"

"We initially received a call from the school about the children running off campus instead of waiting in the car pick-up area. After driving around the neighborhood, we found them attempting to break into a home. The kids said they thought they were at home, but when the school provided us with your address, they were a few streets away from home. Is there a reason why they ran from the school?"

"My hus—their father usually picks them up every day. I don't know why they left the school without permission. As you can see, I'm still working by the time they leave school. His job is more flexible than mine, so he drops them off and picks them up daily," I explained. "Can I go to my desk to get my phone? I need to call him to figure out where he is. He knows he's supposed to get them. Maybe he got caught up with work or something." I spoke the excuse aloud to give myself a logical explanation for his negligence of our children.

"Yes, but before you go... the neighbor whose home they had gotten into... he pulled out a weapon on them. It wasn't fired, but he was justified in protecting himself and his property," Officer Luma explained somberly.

Tears rushed to the surface as I nodded my understanding.

"My kids had a gun pointed at them?" I mumbled with quivering lips.

"I'm so sorry, ma'am."

Rushing out of the conference room, I bypassed the officer guarding my children, and they all rushed to me, wrapping their arms around me.

"I'm so sorry, babies," I cried. Thoughts of the absolute worst-case scenario plagued my mind, from identifying my children's bodies at the morgue to planning their final outfits. I squeezed them tighter.

"Are y'all okay?" I asked, not wanting to let them go, but I wanted to look each of them over individually.

"Yes, Mommy," Kambrel quickly responded. "We thought

it was our house. It's grey and white, just like ours. It wasn't on purpose," he explained, choking back his tears.

"I know, baby... I know." Hugging each of them one more time, I told them to wait in the lobby for me to grab my belongings. I planned to text my supervisor about my situation since he was at training today.

Making my way back to my cubicle, I noticed Caroline moving things around on my desk as if she were looking for something.

"What the fuck are you doing?" I spoke loud enough for the entire floor to hear me.

Heads popped up from various cubicles to see what the commotion was.

"I know you stole it! Where did you put it, Kaila? And don't lie to me. You young heffas are sneaky. Where is my report? Are you trying to make me miss my deadline? Are you trying to get me fired?" In a flustered tone, she continued shoveling papers around my desk, searching for something that wasn't there.

"Caroline, I'm going to say this one time and one time only. If I have to repeat myself, I swear to God you will be leaving on a stretcher." Her movements ceased as she glared, eyes daring me to say something she didn't like. "I need you to get away from my desk. If you don't take heed to this warning, I promise it's going to take the jaws of life to get me off you."

"You don't have to raise your voice at me like that, Miss Moffett. Don't worry. I'll see you tomorrow, and you better have my stuff. You probably took it to your house to be nasty and get me in trouble, but don't worry, I got a trick for that," she grumbled as she strolled away from my desk.

Using my key to unlock the drawer where I kept my personal belongings, I gathered my things, shut down my computer, and headed for the exit. My supervisor responded with praying words and well wishes for the situation. He encouraged me to take the next day off if need be.

After speaking with the police, they determined that my children were not a threat and that they were ultimately safe in my care, so they were allowed to leave with me. I had Taika using my phone to call Charvo, but the voicemail picked up every time. I racked my brain trying to figure out what he could've been caught up in that had him missing the normal pick-up time to get them.

"Why did y'all run away from the school instead of waiting on Daddy to go through the line?" I asked, not speaking directly to either of them.

"He told us to walk like we did last time," Kambrel responded.

"Last time?" I questioned.

My car swerved into the lane beside me before I calmed my nerves and straightened up.

"We remembered where to go last time, and he left the door unlocked. We had to use the house phone to call him and tell him we were home. I don't know how we got lost this time."

A single tear slid down my cheek. The anger coursing through my body wasn't foreign to me. Charvo had a history of doing fuck shit when it came to me; he was usually good about leaving the kids out of it. But hearing that he had been on bull-shit with my children, who had to be cut out of me, had me ready to knock his fucking teeth down his throat.

"I'm going to take y'all to Auntie Pepper's house for a little bit. Let me see my phone, Taika."

Approaching a red light, I texted my sister to tell her I was going to drop the kids off to her for a little while. Although Pepperann and I weren't blood sisters, we still treated each other as such. We were there to look out for each other through the good times and bad. When one of us may have been short on a bill or two, even days when refrigerators lacked food.

Clicking on the social media app I knew Charvo used the most, I went directly to his page to see if he had posted anything recently. The ring around his picture enlightened me that he had posted his story within the last twenty-four hours. Aside from the usual bullshit manly man shit he posted, the last few videos were uploaded two hours prior, and I could see clearly that he was in a strip club. He recorded a plate of hot wings on his lap while a woman was bent over in front of him, shaking her ass.

Dropping the phone into my lap, I almost slammed on the gas to get to the strip club, but I noticed the light was still red. The moment it changed colors, I flew away from the cars trailing me as I switched lanes to reach my destination. Taking the I-95 southbound entrance, we arrived at Playhouse in record time.

"Stay in the car and lock the doors. As soon as you see me walking to the car, unlock it, Taika. Do you understand me?" I was parked directly in front of the club's entrance since the parking lot was full. For it to be four o'clock in the afternoon, these fuck niggas must've been in there blowing bags on them bitches.

"How much is it?" I asked the lady sitting on a barstool near the entrance.

"Two drinks minimum, no cover charge." The woman waved a metal detector.

When the device alerted as she waved it over my purse, I didn't flinch. "Please don't act like you don't know who the fuck I'm here for. I know he's in here, and he was supposed to pick my kids up from school an hour ago. I will speak to him and then come right back out. I'm not here to fuck up this establishment."

"You good, sis. He's in the far left corner, closest to the stage. Try to make it quick. The boss is busy." She winked before unlatching the red rope from the metal pole, granting me access to the club.

Storming across the carpeted floor, my heart thudded inside my chest as the bass from the speakers rumbled my exterior. Charvo stood and let a band of money fly through the air as the girl on the pole worked her magic. The nigga had a bottle of Belaire in his other hand as if he was at the party of the century.

The darkness of the club helped keep me concealed until I approached his section and pulled my pistol out.

"Pussy nigga, where the fuck my kids at?" I raged, rushing to his space with the gun at my side, but the safety was off.

"K... K... Kaila, what the fuck? Ain't you supposed to be at work?" Charvo stuttered.

"Nigga, where the fuck is my kids if you in here popping bottles and throwing money? GO GET MY FUCKING KIDS, CHARVO!!" The brief pause in the music had all eyes on us.

Security was heading to the section from the dark corners of the club. Char's pleading eyes were begging me to calm the fuck down, but about my kids, I'd take shit to the moon.

"You in this fucking club while our kids had a fucking gun pointed at them! It's taking everything in me not to put a bullet in your puny ass brain. I swear to God, Charvo, fuck you, nigga. You got me and my kids fucked up."

"Kaila, chill the fuck out!" he slurred. "It ain't even that deep. This a business meeting. The kids should be home; I told them to walk." He took a big swig from the bottle, gripping it tighter. A security guard stepped between us, forcing me back a few paces. Getting a good look at Charvo, I realized he was drunk and high off his ass. The nigga claimed it was a business meeting, but I knew he didn't conduct his shit like this.

"Did you not just hear what the fuck I said about our kids, Charvo?"

"I heard you, and you fuckin' trippin', Kaila. We can talk about that shit when I make it home. If I make it." Charvo snatched a pile of money off the table, turned around, and threw it in my face.

The shocked gasps throughout the club seemed louder than the music.

Laughing off the embarrassment, I nodded as I walked out of the club. The security guard I bumped into reached for my gun, but I snatched my arm out of his reach. "I told the girl at the front I ain't come here for all that. I'm out, nigga. Get the fuck out of my way," I spat, sizing the man.

"Shit, let me make sure you get outside." I stepped ahead of him as he escorted me out of the club. The people parted ways, making a clear path for me to leave.

Taika's head popped up in the passenger seat, and I heard the doors unlock as soon as our eyes connected. The security guard hovered around the entrance, watching my every move. Before I got in my car, I quickly scanned the parking lot to find Charvo's car. Shooting the security guard the bird, I pulled away from the front of the club.

Instead of leaving through the closest exit, I drove around the side of the building and waited a few minutes. When I returned to the front of the club, the security guard was nowhere in sight. Easing through the lot, I pulled into a spot that was a few spaces away from Charvo's Camaro. It should've been a clear red flag for me when his ass traded in his SUV for this little ass car like we didn't have three kids.

"I'll be right back."

"I need to pee, Mommy."

"Okay, can you hold it, please, Cadell? Mommy needs to do something really fast."

"I can do it, Mommy."

Grabbing the baseball bat that I kept in my trunk, I swiped the bat at the first thing I saw on Charvo's car, followed by the side mirror, driver's side window, and windshield. Wishing I had something to slash his tires, I figured the small damage I did was more than enough for him to know he had me fucked up whenever he was back in his right mind.

The kids and I arrived at Pepper's house fifteen minutes later, and my adrenaline was still pumping. I blasted Trina's song, "Fuck Boy," on repeat as I drove through the streets of Miami. I usually didn't listen to music with curse words in front of my kids, but my anger was getting the best of me.

Cadell hopped out of the truck as soon as we pulled up. My nephews were throwing the football back and forth in the yard, so I knew the kids would be distracted while I filled Pepper in.

"Come pour your own troubles. I can tell yo' ass is on a different level, and I'm not trying to have us both locked up behind yo' baby daddy." Pepper said, passing me the bottle of liquor.

"Girl... I'm fucking done, Pepper! I'm so done with that nigga. On my mama, it's fuck Charvo and everything the pussy nigga stands for." Pouring the Dusse into the red cup with no chaser, I took two big shots back-to-back before making myself an actual drink. I needed this to help ease my nerves and shake the bullshit Charvo caused.

Finding out he was at a fucking strip club while our kids had a fucking gun pointed at them was my last straw with him. He knew how much they meant to me. I was still trying to process him, instructing them to walk home as if they were old enough to do so. We hadn't even taught them how to get to our house, so I can't understand why the fuck he thought it was a good idea.

"That nigga made the kids walk home while his ass was in the fucking strip club. Pepper, I swear I want to kill his black ass!" I raged.

"Before I speak, do you want to vent or hear my honest thoughts? Let a bitch know because this shit can go either way." Pepperann knocked back a shot of Hennessy and shook it off with no chaser.

"At this point, tell me what the fuck you would do because what I'm doing to and for this nigga ain't working no more. Every time I turn around, it's some bullshit with Charvo. I feel like I can't even breathe too good without the nigga doing some fuck shit." Rubbing my temples to help calm my nerves, I knew Pepper was about to cut into me. My sister was one of the sweetest people I knew, and she never liked hurting other people's feelings, but when it came to me, she knew she could give it to me raw. It was up to me whether I listened or not.

"I know my house isn't big enough for all of us, but for the time being, we can make this shit work. You haven't been happy with that nigga since pre-Covid, sis. After you had Cadell, and his ass went and put that fucking deposit down for you to get surgery without you knowing, that should've been the end for you. Charvo is miserable as fuck with his own life. The nigga been *hustling* since you met him, yet his ass sill has nothing to show for it. He ain't icing you out, and he still ain't buy you a fucking house or a car. The nigga is barely putting anything on the bills. I love you more than life itself, Kaila, but you have to let go of the potential you're holding onto when it comes to him. He's shown the world who he is time and time again. I don't understand how your lenses are still blurry."

Pepper's brows pinched together as she nibbled her bottom lip.

She was staring directly at me, shaking her head, but I didn't dare look at her. I knew the well would open, and the endless tears would begin to flow. After all my years of crying for him, I didn't even know how I still had any tears left to give.

"I know... I know." I sighed heavily before gulping down my entire drink.

The cognac burned going down, but it was a welcomed feeling. That burn reminded me of the fire that had been put out of me years ago, my desire for a better life for me and my kids. Everything Pepper said was right; that nigga hasn't done anything for me or my kids to make our lives better. Our oldest was seven years old, yet we were still living in the same two-bedroom apartment, and I was driving around in a whip that was on its last leg. "I'm going to get my shit together, Pep. I feel like I've never been this tired or angry with him, so I have to do what I have to do at this point. It's no sense holding on to this when outside of the kids, there's nothing left between us."

My sister pulled me in for a warm embrace, and surprisingly, I didn't cry. I needed both her strength and my own to get through this, and I knew she'd have my back every step of the way.

"Come on in this kitchen and help me make plates for the kids while we figure out your next move. Like I said, I know it will be tight, but y'all are more than welcome here. We can clear the back room, and I can let the guest bedroom go. We'll do what we have to do to make it work, boo."

"I think we'll be good, sis. I've been dumb over that nigga, but I haven't lost all my sense. My rainy day fund is fully loaded, thanks to his ass, and ready for me to make a move. It's some townhouses I've had my eye on for a while now. I'll go by there before the week is out. Charvo claimed he had a business meeting at the club, so I'm sure he'll be out of the loop in the coming days. I'll have my shit together while he's out of pocket."

"That sounds even better to me. Whatever you need from me, I got you," Pepper said as she started taking plates out of the cabinet for us to feed the kids.

I pulled out my phone to see if I had any missed notifications; there were text messages and phone calls that went unanswered due to my phone being on *Do Not Disturb*. Charvo's thread was at the top of my list, with an image waiting for me. I was sure it would be an apology or a screenshot filled with bullshit of him explaining himself, but I almost dropped my phone, gasping at the picture.

"What the hell—" Pepper stopped what she was doing and walked over to where I sat.

Charvo: All you have to do is say yes, baby. I know I've been fucking up, but I promise I'm doing what I have to do to get our family right.

The diamonds on the engagement ring danced like water in the image. My eyes were wide, and my mouth parted as I was stunned into silence.

CHAPTER TWO
TYREE ROMAN

"Does the twenty-second work for you? I'll be out of the country for ten days. I can change the appointment if need be." Using her Apple Pencil, Starja tapped the screen before her, shuffling back and forth between her business and personal calendars.

"I'll be on break starting the twenty-first, so I can take her to the appointment if you need me to," Vanessa, my other baby's mother, interjected. I listened as the two of them went back and forth, discussing dates, times, and events the kids had coming up that we all needed to add to our calendars.

Once a month, we had a recurring lunch meeting to discuss schedules for our children. It had taken over five years for us to get to a place where we could all sit down like one big, happy family, but those hard times were worth it. Starja, my first baby mother, had my first blessing, Shariyah. Shariyah was heavily involved in track and robotics, so I knew she would succeed with whatever she pursued. Starja and I dated briefly in high school but disconnected shortly after graduation. We connected when she was on a girl's trip in NOLA, and I was out there on business. Ten months later, our princess made her grand entrance.

On the other hand, Vanessa and I were supposed to be in a situation with no strings attached. Whenever she needed the lining knocked out of her pussy, I was the nigga she called. I broke her off with consistent dick and a few dollars in her purse to keep shit sweet between us. By the time she found out she was pregnant with my junior, Starja was weeks away from delivering Shariyah, and she was past the point of terminating the pregnancy.

Initially, I tried keeping the women away from each other to keep the drama and bullshit down, but our situation hit a head when they both started asking for something I didn't want. As much as I loved my children, being with their mothers was never something I wanted long-term. Although we connected sexually, I felt that was the extent of both relationships. Outside of these once-a-month lunch dates, we hadn't been on dates or anything on that level. I kept shit cordial, remained active and present for my kids, and did my best to keep the mothers of my children stress-free.

"What do you have going on out the country? You got your hotel and shit taken care of?" I asked Starja, setting my phone down on the table.

"I had to find a new vendor. The last shipment came in damaged, and they gave me a hard time getting my money back. The boutique was losing customers—there was a lot going on. The quality was worsening, and shipping times were delayed. They started doing bad business overall because of new management. I'm good, though. Everything is already in place." Starja winked.

"Cool, I got you, though. Bring me back something nice." I smirked. "Do you need anything from me, Vanessa?"

My second baby mama, the middle school guidance counselor, had the strength of a million men and the patience of a saint. I urged her to get out of teaching to pursue something else that would make her happy, but she always stressed that working with high school kids was her passion. I was ready to help fund her opening her own school, but she claimed it would be too much work and something she wasn't ready for. I would give it a few more years before circling back to try and sway her. I wanted nothing more than for those two women to elevate their lives for the betterment of our children and themselves. Happy mothers made happy children, and I knew my jits were happy as hell in real life.

"I'm good, Tyree. Spring break is coming up, so I'm counting down. I want to take Shariyah with us on a cruise if that's fine with y'all. TJ's spoiled ass chose a cruise over our usual Disney trip."

Starja and I looked at each other, answering the question without discussing it. "I'll ensure her suitcase is packed before my trip to Nairobi."

Excusing myself from the table when my phone rang, I stepped outside the restaurant to take the call. Ashonte knew what I was doing at the moment, but I answered in case there was an emergency at home.

"What time are you coming back home, baby? I miss you," Ashonte whined.

"I don't hear police sirens or the fire alarm going off. What's up, Ashonte? I'm still with my kids' mothers."

"It's been two hours, Tyree. Ain't that much to talk about. Not much has changed since you met with them last month." The attitude in her squeaky ass voice always pissed me off.

I cared for Ashonte deeply, but certain traits about her had transformed over the last year, and instead of our relationship getting better, we were swimming in the deep end with no life jackets. At times, I felt like she was intentionally trying to push me away to force me to give her what she wanted, but she knew I wasn't making plays out of her book.

"The invite was open to you, Ashonte, but as usual, you declined. I'll be home once I wrap this up and make a few moves."

"What time will that be? I have to head to the shop around three. Can you rush home before you do what you have to do?"

"I can't, Ashonte. What's the issue? I need you to speak and tell me what the fuck is going on because you're dancing around some shit right now. If I can resolve it before we get off the phone without me coming home, let me do that. But if you want me to come home to lay up, it's gotta wait."

"Just go, Tyree. I bet if I were one of those fat-ass baby mamas of yours, you'd come running. And I'm not making dinner tonight, so feed yourself!" Ashonte barked before ending the call.

Disrespecting the mothers of my children was something she would never do in my face, and she knew it. Instead of calling her back to check her on some ignorant shit, I'd deal with her ass whenever I made it home tonight.

"When are you going to let that weird ass bitch go? We're tired of seeing our baby daddy stressed out every time you talk to her," Starja quipped while Vanessa laughed.

"I just don't understand how he got caught up with her skinny ass. She's far from his type. Ain't that right, girl?" The two of them slapped hands while clowning me and my dumbass decision to fuck with Ashonte.

It was no secret I had a thing for big women. My mother and grandmother had no shame in being larger than life, and they made that shit look effortless. Trying to be on some different shit, I gave Ashonte a chance to get right with me, but she was proving to be one of my biggest headaches.

"Just invite us to the wedding." Starja giggled, and I shot her the bird.

After placing our food and drink orders, we continued to catch up on what the kids had been doing for the last few weeks. I enjoyed those moments with my kids' mothers because they allowed me to see different sides of them. They were comfortable around each other, and I was sure they spent time together outside our usual meetings.

"There is something I need to talk to y'all about. I wanted to wait a little longer, but no time like the present." Vanessa used the dinner cloth and the camera on her phone to clean her face. Based on Starja's look, I peeped that she already knew what time it was.

Loosening the tie on my neck and sliding back a bit from the table, I gave Vanessa my undivided attention. She momentarily shuddered under my glare but quickly composed herself before speaking. Starja grabbed her glass and sat back in her seat with a smirk; she was ready for a show.

"Well, I've been seeing someone for a while now, and I would like you to meet him. I haven't brought him around TJ yet, but he does know about him. I've already—"

"Set it up, and I'll be there," I interjected.

"You don't—just like that?"

"I mean, you gotta live, baby. Don't let me hold you back. I appreciate you bringing it to me before you let him around our son. If you feel like he'll be good for you, I'm all for what makes you happy."

Vanessa smiled at my words. I could tell this had been something she was battling with, and it was beginning to weigh her down.

"As always, I appreciate y'all for sitting down to break bread with me. I blessed the accounts. If y'all need something before next month, holla at me. I got you before you catch that flight, Starja. It's always love."

"Yeah, yeah, yeah," Vanessa brushed me off.

"Be safe, baby daddy, and don't forget to send us the wedding invites." Starja kissed my cheek as they walked out of the restaurant, arm-in-arm.

Typically, I would handle my business and square away any loose ends before returning home, but I felt that Ashonte had been a bit too anxious. She never pressed me on my whereabouts. I knew I needed to meet up with my nigga Keem on some business shit he hit my line about, but he'd understand me needing to see about my bitch before getting up with him.

The townhome in North Miami I shared with Ashonte was one of the few I owned. I was hesitant about her moving in with me initially because we got serious quicker than I would've liked, but she was desperate about needing a place to stay, and I knew I was in a position to help her out, so I took care of it.

On the days and nights I spent with my kids, we stayed in our two-story single-family home in Coconut Grove. I liked keeping them as far away from the grimy parts of Dade County as possible, so their moms had no problem staying where I decided it was best for them to live. I hadn't allowed Ashonte to meet my kids yet, and I didn't plan to do so anytime soon. When she met their mothers and showed her natural ass, I should've cut her ass off immediately, but I let her make it. Her ass was too unhinged to be around my children and very much set in her ways. Before I introduced her to the most important aspect of my life, I needed her to get herself together. It took Ashonte a while to get used to me being away while with my kids, and a nigga was constantly getting accused of being on bullshit, but I wasn't budging on my decisions when it came to my children.

A Barbie pink Jeep and an older Mercedes sat in my driveway, blocking my spot. Ashonte knew I didn't like her friends knowing where we laid our heads, so I prepared myself to walk into some bullshit. After parking near the curb in front of my own fucking crib, I noticed the front door was cracked as I approached, and I could hear the women inside talking loudly like they were at a fucking party or some shit. It was after three o'clock on a Tuesday. Why weren't these bitches at work?

"Damn, bitch, you ain't got nothing to eat in here? I haven't eaten shit all day, so my stomach would be flat for this shoot, but my ass is about to pass the fuck out."

The kitchen was close to the foyer. Standing in the right position, I could see directly into the kitchen without anyone noticing me.

The woman was ass naked with my subzero refrigerator wide the fuck open like she couldn't see through it with the door closed.

"Ohh, fuck, I'm about to cum again!!"

Loud moaning forced me out of the foyer and into the direction of the noises. I couldn't say I was shocked about the scene I had walked into. I had a feeling she was on some sneaky shit. Ashonte's face was covered with a bright yellow ski mask, and she was bent over while a bitch was hitting her from the back with a strap-on. Her ass was moaning and groaning like she was getting fucked with the real thing. Another broad stood behind them with an expensive ass camera, recording the entire scene.

My presence didn't seem to gain attention from anyone. Instead of speaking, I walked up to the camera and smacked that shit to the ground. Tiny pieces scattered about the floor, and the stand was no longer functioning.

"What the fuck?" the woman blurted out, causing Ashonte's eyes to lock with mine as her fear surfaced.

When I glared at the woman, she quickly looked away and started scanning the floor to pick up the pieces of her camera.

"Tyree! What are you doing here, baby? I thought you had a meeting or something?" Ashonte approached me with her hands extended as if she were about to grab me. The simple raise of an eyebrow halted her movements.

"I'm not interested in shit you have to say, Ashonte. I don't know what the fuck y'all got going on, but if y'all not out of my shit in the next two minutes, ain't nobody walking out of that door."

"Ty—"

"Say my name, and I'll break your fucking face. You and all these hoes can get her fuck out of my crib! Ain't shit to talk about."

"Give me a minute to get my stuff."

"If you don't have a receipt for anything in this house, I suggest you get the fuck out of here with the bullshit you got on right now. Play with me if you want to, Ashonte. In my shit making fucking porn and shit—bitch you lost yo' rabid ass mind." I scoffed, shaking my head.

"Fuck you, Tyree! I'm going to get my clothes. You not gonna stand here and tell me what the fuck to do. Nigga, you not my daddy. If you were a real nigga and breaking bread, I wouldn't have to do any shit like this to make ends meet. I'm supposed to be a paid bitch, not out here begging you for time, money, or attention!" Ashonte screamed as she shed a few tears.

"Thirty seconds," I said, checking the time on my watch.

"I'm not going nowhere, Tyree. This is my motherfucking house, too, and I can do what I want when I want. If you want me to leave, you gonna have to put me out."

The other women had cleared the scene as I mentally counted down their final ten seconds. Ashonte glanced at me after hearing the front door slam shut. Naked and all, those bitches got the fuck on. I didn't understand why she didn't understand that I wasn't bullshitting.

Taking my time to get to the front door, I stopped at the small side table to set down my keys, phone, and wallet before leaving the door wide open. I wasn't about to play with this bitch.

"Tyree, please. Just let me explain, baby! Hear me out.... I just needed to make some money. Business has been slow... Tyree..."

Lifting her off her feet and tossing her over my shoulder, she kicked and punched wildly as I took purposeful steps to the front door.

Since my truck was blocking her friends from leaving, I continued out the door and stopped when I made it to the ugly-ass jeep in my spot.

"If you don't let me go, I promise we gon' hit this hot ass ground together. Be a woman about your shit, Ashonte. You fucked around and found out." In one swift motion, her body was on the hood of the jeep as she cried loudly. I knew her naked ass had to be burning under this hot-ass Miami sun but fuck her.

———

Keem was kicked back in a section at Takeoff, one of the many businesses we owned together. When I decided to get out of the game four years ago, I took the time to invest in my future to make sure I had shit locked down for my jits. I knew that drug and gun shit had a guaranteed expiration date if I didn't make a move before my number was called. Keem had been the only nigga on my team who was ready and willing to step up and make the necessary plays. Although I was out, he kept me updated on the comings and goings of the business.

"Look at this nigga, man! Boy, yo' ass needs to get your weight back up. Big ass shirt, little ass pants. I know Ashonte's ass still not shaking them pots and pans up on a regular." Keem talked shit as he dapped me up.

"Fuck you, nigga. That's what we got Starja for."

"Shit, she was supposed to be my baby mama first, nigga!" Keem jabbed.

"You wish, mother fucker." That nigga always joked about wanting to be one of Starja's baby daddies, especially since he knew I wasn't locking her ass down.

Years ago, I gave him the green light to snatch her up, but she shot him down without a second thought. Loyalty was at the root of her heart, even though shit was never that deep between her and me. I respected the fact that she respected enough to not entertain the nigga.

"You want to go to the office? Want some wings or something? That nigga Troy back in the kitchen making them good ass wing boils."

"Nigga, the fuck I look like eating a fucking boil? Just get me some hot wings fried hard and extra sauce. Tell that nigga don't be giving them little ass wings either. I want my shit whole."

Keem got up and headed to the kitchen while I sat down to pour myself a drink. After downing it quickly, I poured another one and did the same. The bullshit with Ashonte still had me ready to spaz the fuck out, but I knew I needed to keep shit cool. Keem was my nigga, but I didn't like discussing the shit Ashonte and I had going on. He couldn't care less about her crazy ass, so I rarely gave him the green light to share his thoughts on her.

"What you got going for it? What's the move? Let me know something. I ain't drive out here after dealing with Ashonte's scheming ass for nothing." I got at Keem when he sat back down with his burner phone.

The facial expression he wore was one that I didn't think I'd seen too many times before. My nigga looked like he was stressed, and his lights would get cut off at any second.

"I need you, nigga. I fucked up." Keem shrugged as he plopped down on the seat beside me. He snatched the bottle of 1800 off the small table in front of him and knocked the bottle back, taking large gulps of the burning liquid. Releasing a loud breath and then a belch, I knew this nigga was drunk, so whatever he needed to lay on me would be raw.

"I'm out for a reason, Keem," I reminded him, my eyes catching my favorite bottle girl as she emerged from one of the side rooms.

Locking eyes with me, her single eyebrow rose, and my slight head nod alerted her to my current need. I knew she would have me taken care of in a matter of moments.

"Just help me get this shit together, then I promise I won't ask you to do this again." Keem faced me with pleading eyes.

"What the fuck happened, nigga?"

"Some nigga they call Green ran through the spots. He hit two of them shits on the same fucking day, nigga. The thing is, he ain't even from down here, but he does have people here. Nigga from the O, so I don't know how he got the drop on the way this shit moving down here."

"It ain't never a you don't know. You know... you need to figure out who's leaving that cheese trail. Don't tell me yo' ass done got so motherfucking comfortable that you forgot how shit works. You feed a nigga today. He'll rock yo' taco tomorrow. You feel me?"

Keem ran a hand down his stressed face. I could tell he

didn't want to have to call on me to help him out of this shit. What grown man wanted to admit to needing another grown man to help him get his shit together?

"What's the move, nigga? If we need to take a trip to Orlando, say the word."

CHAPTER THREE
CHARVO HARRIS

"Come fuck with me, nigga. I got so much shit up here, I don't know what the fuck to do with it," Green chirped through the phone.

The nigga was my blood cousin, but I couldn't trust him as far as I could toss his ass. Gerald's nickname, Green, was more than fitting because he was always on some snake shit. A few nights ago, he hit my phone to make a play, but Kaila and the kids had me caught up, so I was out of pocket.

Word on the street was the nigga hit up some lame-ass goofy nigga who had left the shit sitting out for him. Green ain't even have to drop a body to run through that shit.

"Shit, let me put something in motion. You know Kaila has been on my ass. Man, I gotta come up with something good to get out the fucking dog house and make this play," I urged.

"You know I don't get down with bitches trying to lock a nigga down, so I ain't got nothing for you. If you get some shit together in the next day or so, hit my line."

"Bet that up," I responded before ending the call.

My mind was already working overtime to figure out how

to tell Kaila I needed to slide to the O for a few days. The fact that she was pissed at me for telling the kids to walk home was the least of my worries; her putting a stop motion on me getting to some paper presented a more significant issue.

"Do you need anything else? My shift is about to end, and I need all my tabs closed out." The bottle girl, Alexia, was straightening the table in the middle of the section or at least pretending to while trying to get at my pockets.

"I paid for all my shit." I shrugged, not looking away from my phone.

While scrolling through Google, I was trying to find the perfect picture to send to Kaila. I knew this would stir the pot, but it was all I could think of to get her off my back for a few days. The perfect picture was on Instagram of all places. I screenshotted a man holding a ring box, and his hand looked similar to mine, so I had to make it work.

I didn't give the text message I sent much thought because I knew once she saw the ring, all the negative emotions would dissipate. Kaila had been breathing down a nigga's back to propose to her ass, so she better be happy with this shit and shut her ass up. Our kids ain't that fucking small for her to be showing her ass and popping up on a nigga when I just needed a moment to myself.

"I don't like how you act like you don't know me no more, Charvo, but it's all good," Alexia whined as I stood, prepared to walk out of the section and leave the club.

"It's always love, shawty. It would help if you remembered your position. If you ever see my bitch, you make yourself disappear. Niggas killing bitches over nothing these days, and if you fuck up my family, you'll be another statistic, baby."

"Whatever, nigga. You ain't even happy with the bitch, so I don't know why you are keeping up this facade."

"Watch yo' mouth," I warned. "Listen, I might need you to

make a move with me to Orlando for a few days. I got some plays to run and shit. You know I need you beside me to get shit done the right way."

"I told you last time that I was done with that shit. I almost got popped behind yo' dumbass."

"You always bringing up old shit, Alexia. Hit my line tomorrow so we can make this move. After this, I promise you'll be able to kick your feet up and never work another day in your life."

"Oh, you on that type of time?"

"You know how I get down. Lose the attitude; you know I get you right every time."

"Yeah, yeah, yeah, nigga. I'll holla." She rolled her eyes as she left the section.

Walking out of the strip club, I noticed a small group of people standing too fucking close to my car. I got my shit detailed this morning. I'd be pissed if I saw a fucking fingerprint on it. As I neared the vehicle, I started feeling sick to my stomach, and my head was spinning.

"Who the fuck did this shit to my whip?" I raged, breaking through the small crowd to survey the damage. Three slashed tires, both front and back windshield busted out, key marks from bumper to bumper... this shit had a nigga weak in the knees.

"That nigga pissed somebody off!" I heard someone from the gaggle say, but I disregarded their comment. I couldn't take my eyes off my Camaro.

My phone rang in my hand, and I immediately hit the decline button without seeing who was calling. Whatever it was and whoever it was needed to wait. As soon as I got the incoming call off the screen, I opened the app for my insurance company and clicked through the prompts to request roadside assistance.

When the notification alerted me that there would be a three to four-hour wait, I headed back inside the club to speak with one of the managers. I didn't want to sit out there and wait for my car to get picked up, so I went in to ensure it would be cool for me to leave instead of waiting.

After securing everything I needed, I got an Uber to take me home since Kaila wasn't answering the phone for me. I thought she'd beat down my line once she received the ring picture, but I was sadly mistaken. The way my calls went straight to voicemail and my text messages kept saying 'undelivered,' I felt that my efforts had been pointless.

"You can stop right here, man," I told the Uber driver before he approached my house.

In the distance, I saw Pepper's baldheaded ass carrying a heap of clothes to her trunk before turning around and going back inside my house.

"Hurry up, Kaila. That nigga is probably on his way, and I'm not in the mood to be fighting tonight," Pepper yelled loud enough for the entire block to hear her.

"Whatever y'all think y'all got going on is dead. Where the fuck is Kaila, and why the fuck are taking shit out of my house?" My voice echoed through the space, startling Pepper.

"Nigga, fuck you! This ain't your fucking house. Yo' ass can't even afford a fucking house, broke ass bitch." Pepper's words cut into me.

"See, I should snatch yo' ass up..."

"Put your hands on my sister, and we'll both beat your ass. Let me get the rest of what I need for the kids and me, and then we'll be on our way."

"Where are you going, Kaila? I ended my business meeting early to come home and celebrate with you. A nigga just proposed, and this is the fucking thanks I get?"

"Show me the ring, Charvo."

"It's—"

"Show it to me right now. I don't want to hear no fucking excuses," Kaila snapped.

"Can we talk without a fucking audience? I'm trying to tell you what's happening with the ring. I told you I know I've been fucking up. I'm trying to get us right, baby. Please hear me out."

"This nigga is so full of shit, sis. I told you! You got the screenshot, so I don't know why you're sitting here, willing to hear him out. Clown ass fuck nigga," Pepper's rude ass interjected.

"Did you get that picture off Instagram?" Kaila asked, and I could feel the sweat beading on my forehead.

"Kaila—"

"Yes or fucking no, Charvo!! It ain't that hard." Kaila was speaking to me like a mad woman. I wondered if my last stunt had pushed her to that position of being fed up like the old-school R&B singers used to warn us about.

"The ring is in Orlando, Kaila. I planned a surprise trip to Disney World, and I wanted to do the shit up there. I got a jeweler up there who handmade the piece just for you. I got the shit engraved and everything. A nigga was going out of his way to make shit romantic for yo' ass, but you not being patient with me. I only want you, Kaila, and I want to do this shit the right way. I'm trying to do right by you and our kids. Fuck all the outside noise and the fuck ups I've made in the past. I'm done with all the games and little boy shit. I'm ready to stand in the paint and be a man about my shit. But I don't want to do this without you by my side.

"Kaila, please forgive me for that shit earlier. I wasn't trying to put the kids in harm's way. Honestly, they've walked home a few times, and it was no issue. I'll accept that this shit is all my fault. I'll accept that I haven't been the man you need me to be for you or our kids. I see the error in my ways, and I'm willing to put in the work to make this shit better for all of us. I got a down payment for the house and a five-day family vacation paid for. All you have to do is say yes, baby. I swear to God, I got us from here on out." I was kneeling in front of Kaila, pleading for her not to give up on me. I knew I could be more than the nigga she needed me to be.

I hated being the reason she had tears falling from her eyes and a heart torn into so many pieces. I wanted to do right by her. All I needed was one more chance.

"I need time, Charvo." Kaila sniffled. "Give me a few days to myself so we can figure out where to go from here."

"We have to leave for the trip on Thursday. If you decide this is what you want, pack your bags so we can get on the road around noon. I love you so much, Kaila. From the bottom of my heart, I'm sorry for all the hurt I've caused you. I can be a better man. Give me a chance to show you."

"She said she needs time, Charvo. Get yo' stupid ass up and out of her way." Pepper grabbed Kaila by the arm, and they left the living room.

I could hear Kaila telling Pepperann what to grab out of the kids' room, and then, in less than five minutes, they were gone.

A nigga wasn't perfect, but I never thought I'd see the day my bitch gave up on me. How deep could she say her love was for me if she folded at the first sign of adversity?

———————

The vibrating of my phone against the nightstand was pissing me off. I felt like I had just laid down and closed my eyes. Now, someone was blowing down my line nonstop. Snatching my phone, I ripped the charger out of the block and hit the small lamp, which almost tumbled to the ground but got caught against the mattress instead. I was about to switch my phone to 'do not disturb,' but seeing my mom's name scroll across the top of the screen, I knew it had to be an emergency. It was almost three in the morning, so I knew she wasn't calling to make small talk.

"Why the fuck do we have to call you a hundred times for you to answer the phone, Charvo? Get yo' black ass up and get over here right the fuck now!" I heard screaming in the background and the faint sounds of police sirens.

"I'm sleep, Ma."

"Well, wake the fuck up. Clarissa's house got shot up, and I know you know what the fuck this is about."

"How am I supposed to know what that's about if I just told you I'm at home sleeping?"

"Say something else, and I'm knocking those big, fake ass teeth out yo' mouth. Get here now, Charvo!"

Like a child throwing a tantrum when they don't get what they want, I flung the comforter off my body and then went into the bathroom to get myself together.

"Yo!" I called out to the sleeping figure in my bed when I peeked out of the bathroom.

"Why are you yelling so loud, nigga? It's three in the morning."

"You gotta go. I have to make a move. Get up and get your shit," I told her, knowing she was playing sleep. Her nosey ass was moving around while I was on the phone with my mom.

"I can ride with you. I don't want to go back home yet."

"Sounds good, but that's not what we doing. I'll hit you when I get back in town."

"When are you leaving? You didn't tell me anything about this. See, this is exactly why I don't like dealing with you. It's always everything on your time and how you want it. You don't give a fuck about me, Charvo. I'm already going through a lot. Why do I have to deal with bullshit from you too?"

"Do any of these pictures hanging up on my walls resemble you? I don't give a fuck about what you have to deal with. Shit ain't ever been that deep between us, so pipe the fuck down. Yo' ass shouldn't be here anyway. If my wife and kids walked in this bitch, I'm sure she would kill both of us in our sleep," I barked.

Walking to my dresser, I grabbed the first pair of sweatpants I saw, along with a wife beater and a pair of black socks. Sliding my feet into my Crocs, I stopped what I was doing when I noticed she hadn't moved from the bed.

"A—"

"I'm leaving, Charvo. Give me a fucking minute. I'm requesting a ride," she spat and slowly started getting out of bed.

"Don't leave no panties, earring backs... nothing. You tried to be slick last time, but I found the shit. You're welcome!" I huffed.

"Fuck you! I hope she catches your ass soon. You can't keep me a secret forever."

"Bet?" I challenged, and she shot the bird at me.

The car she requested pulled up in less than ten minutes, and I was kind enough to walk her outside since it was the middle of the night.

The old unused Altima I bought Kaila years ago sat in the driveway, and as I made my way toward it, I prayed it would do me right when I went to my aunt's house. Since she upgraded herself to a Suburban, we only cranked up the Altima occasionally and went around the block a few times to ensure it was still in working condition.

Like a charm, it cranked easily, and I was headed to Broward to see about my people. I did not know how the car would do on I-95, so I took 441 to Sunrise Boulevard, catching all green lights. After making a few turns and bending a few corners, the police lights and caution tape drew me directly to the scene of the action.

I parked as close as I could to my aunt's house before tucking my pistol under the seat and getting out. The commotion seemed to have died down from when my mom initially called me, and there weren't too many people standing outside being nosey.

My mom was sitting on the trunk of her car, sipping out of a red cup, while my aunt sat next to her with her head in her hands.

"What they talking about, Ma?" I asked, approaching them.

"Are you really going to stand here and act like you don't know what this is about? Them niggas tried to kill my sister! Where the fuck is your cousin because they left a message for his ass?" my mom fumed.

"I don't know what's going on. Green hit my phone saying he was down here, and the next thing I knew, he was calling and saying he's back in the O. I ain't been with him. Me and Kaila got some shit going on. I've been home with her and the kids." It was a partial truth but still more than enough for her to know that I wasn't with that nigga while he was in town.

"They dropped off a piece of my dead daughter's headstone, Charvo. What the fuck are y'all into? What the fuck did he do this time? Who did he fuck over?" Aunt Clarissa was in tears. I could hear the heartbreak in her voice as she spoke to me.

"I don't—" My mother gave me a single look that halted my words. This was one of those times I hated that I had lied so much in the past.

Mom hugged Aunt Clarissa as I stood back and watched.

My little cousin Monica was caught in the crossfire of a drive-by shooting when she was eleven years old. The shit happened when Green and I were jumping off the porch at eighteen, and till this day, it still fucked with me. Every time somebody was ready to get at that nigga, someone else got hurt in the process. A can of oil ain't have shit on him.

Once my mom got Aunt Clarissa to calm down, she pulled me aside to speak privately. I braced myself for the tongue lashing that I knew she was about to serve me.

"Whatever you have to do to fix this," with a finger, she motioned to my aunt, her home, and the block she lived on, "fix it. I don't want to hear any excuses. I don't want to listen to any more fucking lies from you, Charvo. I'm sick of it. I don't want to have to bury my sister behind you and your cousin. We told y'all to keep that street shit far away from us, but now the shit is literally at her doorstep. Do you understand me, Charvo?"

I was fixing my mouth to explain myself one more time, but the glare she was sending let me know that she would knock me in my shit if I said something other than, "Yes, ma'am, I understand."

CHAPTER FOUR
ASHONTE NEGRON

"Why are you acting so scared now, Ashonte? Just post it. The cat is out of the bag, and we need to get into ours. The nigga knows now, and it ain't like he yo' damn daddy." Barbie stood on the other side of the kitchen island, making herself a drink as I listened to her rant.

She had been tap dancing on my nerves since Tyree kicked us out of the house. His ass was supposed to be out handling business, not popping up and stopping motion. Although Tyree catered to every single want and need I could ever have. Lately, I felt like I wasn't getting enough from him, so I devised a plan to get it on my own. I never wanted to work another day in my life, and I couldn't imagine what he didn't understand about that. I figured making and posting videos on a private account could bring in money for our small team. However, I didn't expect to get caught in the midst of the very first video.

I promised the girls that we could use my place since it looked the best aesthetically, and my house was clean. The plan was to get multiple scenes around the house, but when Tyree walked in, we had only managed to get three scenes done. Next time, I would go with my first mind and rent a house for us to do this shit. I was embarrassed as hell when he kicked all of us out with three of us ass-naked, but thankfully, Barbie managed to grab our bags on the way out, so we got dressed in the car.

"Can you chill on me? He might not be my daddy, but the nigga does take care of me," I countered while slowly scrolling through Tyree's Instagram to see if I needed to check one of the thirsty bitches trying to get at him.

"If he was taking care of you, why the fuck did you suggest us making that video? You were the one who had the fucking idea, Ashonte. Now, Bugs's camera is fucked up, Crystal can't go home to that nigga without her bread, and bitch, you got me fucked up if you think I'm out here fucking for free. This shit is going one of two ways, so you better choose wisely." She quickly swiped my phone from my hand, forcing me to give her my undivided attention. "Then the bitch is sitting here on social media. Girl, are you even listening to what I'm saying?"

"I heard you. I'm not a child, Barbie. Give me my phone. I'm trying to come up with a plan for us to post this and for me to keep my man. I'm not an independent bitch like you. I don't have a pimp like Crystal, and I don't know what the hell Bugs got going on, but my life is nothing like hers. I got a nigga who goes through hell and high waters to make me happy. I don't even know why y'all listened to me when I was talking that shit, anyway. I was high as fuck." I scoffed.

"I'm not hearing any of that. Either we post the video at 8:00 tonight or first thing in the morning, Tyree will know all about that little booger-nose brat you got running around this city in them too tight ass shoes. Do I make myself clear?"

"Barbie, come on, now. Why would you do that? That's low, even for you."

"I can get lower if you'd like."

"Fuck you. At least I can have kids, hoe. I didn't run to the clinic, unlike you." I grabbed my purse off the counter to storm out of the kitchen, but Barbie rushed around the island before I got too far.

"Oh, but who's taking care of yo jit, Ashonte? You call yourself a mom, but you go to sleep every night, not knowing if your child ate or not. I'd rather get rid of it than bring it into this world, knowing I'm not mentally or physically ready for what real motherhood comes with."

"If I judged you for all your mishaps and hangups, we would be here all day. Keep my jit's name out yo mouth and know that you not checking me about a fuck thing. When I call the play, we'll make the move. I'm not risking my livelihood for y'all broke asses."

"Regarding my money, that's a play you can't call. You might think you know me, but I promise you, you're about to know me on a different level if the funds aren't hitting my account come sunrise." Pressing her finger in the center of my forehead, she mushed my head back.

Reflexively, my purse swung up, hitting her in the face. "Don't you ever in your life put your fucking hands on me. We can go outside and get in the fucking grass if you on that."

"Get your crybaby ass out of here. If I didn't just get my nails done, I would've knocked that ugly ass mop off your head."

"I'm none of these scary ass bitches, Barbie. You ain't threatening shit cuz you ain't shit to be scared of. Like I already said, we're moving when I say move, and if you don't like playing by my rules, you can eliminate the video. You don't know how to use that fucking strap anyway." I rolled my eyes and stepped past her to leave.

I didn't bother speaking to Crystal or Bugs on my way out.

They were too scared to move without Barbie thinking for them, so there wasn't anything else to say.

Instead of waiting around in Barbie's apartment complex, I walked three blocks down to the gas station and requested a Lyft to my mom's house. I needed her to help me figure out how to escape this situation. She was the reason I was with Tyree in the first place, so I needed her to fix this.

"Ashonte?" I heard a woman scream my name as I stood on the curb near the free vacuum and air pump. I scanned the parking lot without looking too bothered because I didn't want to draw attention to myself.

Although this wasn't my side of town, my baby's father, Keith's people, lived around here. It was just my fucking luck that his sister was pulling in to get gas at the pump nearest me.

"Ashonte! I know you hear me, girl. What are you doing over here? Did you call Keith to tell him you were out here?" Shannon asked. She had abandoned her car full of kids to approach me as I stood with my face scrunched due to the sun blaring down on me.

"Nah, I'm not over here for all that. I just left my homegirl's house, and I'm going back home now."

"I know you're not leaving without seeing KJ..." Shannon paused as she sized me.

Shrugging, I felt great relief when I noticed the car described on the Lyft app pulling into the parking lot to pick me up.

"Tell them I said what's up. It was nice seeing you. You look good, boo." I waved my hand so the driver would spot me as I rushed away from Shannon.

As soon as I slammed the car door, I told the driver to pull off. I saw Shannon pulling out her phone and snapping pictures. I was more than sure I'd be hearing from Keith's aggravating ass before the sun went down today.

"Run it back to me one more time, Ashonte. I thought you got your sense from me, but the shit you do makes me remember I laid down with that deadbeat ass nigga to make you." My mother shook her head in disgust as I filled her in on what went down with Tyree and the girls. I expected her to have some profound advice for me or to tell me what I should do to fix what I had gotten myself into, but my mom stared at me like I was an attraction at a circus, letting the balloons fly away.

"I don't think he's that mad at me. He hasn't blocked me on social media or his phone. I still have his location," I quickly explained, feeling like I was grasping at straws.

"The problem with you young girls is y'all live for that social media shit. So what, you have his location? So the fuck what, he hasn't blocked you, Ashonte? Tyree is a great man, and unfortunately, you lost this one, my girl. You wrapped him up in a nice bow for the next woman to take him home and tuck him in. All of that scrolling up and down on social media got your head messed up, and I hate to see you like this. You and I both know he came in and changed your life for the better. Tyree is a man of order. Hell, I don't see him much, but every time I'm around him, I can tell he needs things a certain way before he steps foot into any room.

"What makes you think he's going to continue putting up with your shit and making space for you in his life when this situation alone has made it clear that you're not it for him? You can sit there and cry all you want, but you did this to yourself. I can't even say I wish I could fix this for you. I've told you time and time again to get your shit together with this man. I wish you would've listened a long time ago."

I didn't realize I was crying until she mentioned it, and the tears started dripping onto my white shirt, leaving trails of makeup down my face.

"I'm trying to do right by him but I just—I need more from him. Our lives have become so routine and boring. All he wants me to do is work in my suite, cook and clean for him, be ready to get up and go when he says it, and wait on his beck and call. My life is just passing me by while I'm waiting for him to wake up and realize what he has."

"And what exactly does he have?" Her words caused me to snap my head back. "You can fix your face and answer my question." She stared blankly.

"I just told you... I cook, clean, work when I have clients, and take care of home."

"Okay... and what exactly are you doing to benefit him? You cook because you're also hungry. You clean because you don't want to live in filth, and if we're being honest, you haven't been to that suite in the last month. I have access to the camera system, too. Again, what are you doing to give him peace, to pour into his life, to make his life easier or better as he did yours?"

"Everything I do makes his life better. I know it does. He'll even tell you that."

"So why did you feel the need to disrespect him in the house he owns?"

Sucking my teeth, I was ready to leave. She had soured my mood with her team Tyree speech, and I was sick of hearing it. My mom warned me years ago about keeping a man like Tyree. Although I didn't take all her advice, I picked up a few of the gems she dropped. I felt that I was doing everything I needed to do to keep my man locked in. She didn't know what she was talking about.

I knew Tyree was mad at me, but at least I didn't cheat on

him with another nigga. That was some shit you couldn't come back from.

"There she goes, running off when she doesn't get her way. You're just like your no good ass daddy," my mom grumbled as I left the living room and headed to my old bedroom. She had converted it into a guest room, but I occupied the room whenever I stayed at her house.

I found an old pair of pajamas in one of the bottom drawers and decided to shower before I laid down to figure out my next move. Letting Tyree go was the last thing I was going to do.

After thinking it over for a few minutes, I decided to FaceTime him to see if we could talk. The thump of my beating heart echoed throughout my body and banged loudly in my ears as the phone rang. Surprisingly, he answered before it stopped ringing.

When the line connected, Tyree had the phone facing the roof of his truck, so I couldn't see him.

"Can we talk, baby? Are you mad at me?" With my lip poking out, I stared at the screen, waiting for him to appear.

"Can I get some blackened ranch and extra napkins, shawty? Appreciate you."

"Tyree? Why are you eating that bullshit? Let me come home and make you a home-cooked meal, babe. I can use my mom's car and be there in fifteen minutes."

"What do you want to talk about, Ashonte?" The phone was repositioned to the holder on his dashboard, so I had a clear view of him as he bit into a piping hot biscuit and blew out the hot smoke.

"I'm so sorry, Tyree. I didn't mean for that to go down like that. I needed to make some extra money since business has been slow for me at the salon. That's not something I do all the time; it was my first time. Are you listening to me?" I pouted, watching him rip apart a chicken thigh and stuff his mouth. The Popeyes box rested on his lap as he grabbed fries from it.

"I'm good on you, Ashonte. This shit has been cool, but let's call a spade a spade. I'll set you up in an apartment of your choosing and pay rent for three more months on your suite. Find something you like and can afford, then shoot me the details."

"So, it's over just like that, Tyree?"

"You didn't seem to have a problem with us being over earlier," he said with a mouth full of food.

"Tyree, it wasn't like that."

"So, what the fuck was it like? From the looks of things, you had naked bitches running all up and through my shit like they pay my fucking bills. You, of all people, know how I am about my space, yet you still chose to violate it. You swiped the table clean, baby girl, and now there is nothing else we need to discuss."

"It was a business deal... it's not that deep."

"Not that deep? Answer this one question before we get off the phone. When is the last time you've been at your suite?"

"What does that have to do with anything?" I rebutted.

"Answer my question or get off my line, Ashonte."

"I was there a few days ago. People are not booking like that anymore, Tyree. I told you that business has been slow for me. I was going in every day and only had one or two clients a week. I don't want to keep coming to you with my hands out whenever I need something. I found a solution that would be very profitable. I don't see the problem."

"What's crazy is when I first moved you into that suite, you had consistent business. The problem now is your ass got lazy. You're looking at what all the Instagram hoes got, and you want that lifestyle, not realizing you already have it. But it's cool, Ashonte. That's my bad."

"It's not cool, Tyree. We need to talk about this. We can fix it. I made a mistake—"

"This my ol' girl calling, I gotta go. Don't forget to send the apartment you want. I'll be out of pocket for a few days, but I'll have all your stuff moved out when I return. Stay up, Ashonte." His greasy finger mashed the end button while my mouth hung open, shocked by his revelation. Hearing him say he was done with me shattered my heart. I never thought I'd see the day, and I didn't expect it to come out like this.

CHAPTER FIVE
KAILA MOFFETT

Thursday morning came much quicker than I anticipated, and as I lay in bed at Pepperann's house, I was rethinking my decision to go on the trip with Charvo. Admittedly, I was tired of the constant bullshit that always seemed to find its way into our relationship. I just wanted peace at the end of the day, and as much as I wished Charvo could provide that peace to me and the children, deep in my heart, I knew he couldn't give it to us.

Going into my phone, I went back into Charvo's messages and stared at the engagement ring he sent yesterday. Even though I found out he stole the picture, I wondered if his intentions were real. He knew I wanted marriage, the big, happy family, and the big family house where we hosted for every holiday. The internal battle I was fighting made it more difficult for me to make sound decisions regarding him. Before bringing out the best parts of me, he forced me to reach into the depths of my soul and bring out the beast that I no longer wished to be. I shouldn't feel like I had to go to war with the man I lay beside every night. I knew it wouldn't always be rainbows and butterflies, but I couldn't remember the last time I even felt that the sun was smiling down on us.

I heard the front door open and close before Pepperann's sandals slapped against the tile floor. She made her way into the guest bedroom and peeked in to check on me and the kids.

"Did I wake you?"

"No, I was up. I need to get us together so we can go. I think I'll take the trip and see how it goes." Shifting out of bed without waking the kids, we walked out of the room and into the hallway to talk.

"Kaila, do you think that's a good idea? He won't propose, and I know you know that. Charvo is full of shit, and he's been that way since you met him."

"I hear you, Pepper, but let me figure this out alone. I need to see this through to know if I'm done. And the kids deserve a vacation. That's the least we can take from the nigga before I leave with them for good."

"I don't get you, Kaila. Last night, you moved all your stuff out and talked big shit about being done, but now you sound like you'll give it another chance. I know the heart wants what it wants, but the nigga keeps doing fuck shit, and this time, it involved the kids. He didn't even do anything about that old ass man pulling a gun on them. Don't be too weak for the nigga is all I'm saying."

"I hear you, and I appreciate your advice. At the end of all this, the kids and I will be in our own space, or we'll start planning my wedding in a few weeks." I shrugged.

Pepperann shook her head as she walked away and headed to her bedroom. I noticed she had her purse hanging on her shoulder, but I didn't bother to question where she was returning from. Knowing her, she probably hit the grocery store before it got too busy this morning.

I managed to pack the kids' bags, and we were ready to go.

Pepper cooked us breakfast and wished us well as we left her house. She tried to talk me out of the trip again, but I ignored her as I got in my truck and headed home so we could get on the road.

Charvo had texted me earlier to see if I had decided to go so he could determine what time we'd be getting on the road. As nervous as I was about it, I felt that I needed this. And after what my kids had been through, they deserved a nice family vacation, too.

"Come on, y'all. Change into these clothes so we can take pictures and go." Charvo held family road trip shirts with matching Crocs for all of us as we backed into the driveway. He had the doors open, and the kids rushed out to get to him.

"Daddy got us shirts, Mommy!" Cadell was ecstatic as he jumped out of the truck.

After Charvo hugged and kissed the kids, he sent them inside to change clothes, then came around and opened the driver's side door.

"Thank you, Kaila. I love you for real." Chavo kissed my hand before helping me out of the truck.

"I hear you. Let me go get them together. Did you get a rental?" I asked, looking around the yard.

"We're taking your truck. That's what it's made for. I got the gas, detailing, and everything. Don't stress," he coaxed.

I loved my cocaine white Suburban and knew it was made for large families going on road trips, but I had yet to put my baby on the road for real. I got it less than six months ago, so I was low-key excited to see how it would do on the four-hour drive.

I sat comfortably in the passenger seat as Charvo navigated the vehicle to get our family to Orlando safely. Prior to our departure, he sent me the information for the rental home he had reserved and requested that I look over it to make any special requests. The only options I added were a gas grill and the heat option for the pool. This was going to be a trip to remember.

After riding for only an hour, I noticed Charvo watching the rearview mirror every few seconds. When he sat up in the seat and gripped the steering wheel, I didn't like his concerned expression.

"You good baby?" I turned around to see if someone was possibly driving too close to us, but I didn't see anyone.

"I'm cool. I was thinking about the quote I got to get the Camaro repaired. It's a small thing to a giant, though." He shrugged it off, his eyes lingering in the mirror again before focusing on the road.

He remained silent for a few minutes, seemingly in his thoughts, before announcing that he wanted to stop so the kids could use the bathroom.

"I think they're good. We just got on the road, and I ensured they used the bathroom before leaving. They haven't even had anything to drink since earlier this morning," I countered.

"Just in case, I'm pulling over at the next rest stop," he stressed.

Instead of arguing, I sat back and silently glanced over at him. His energy had shifted, and I prayed this was just a one-off since our trip had just gotten started.

The vacation home was beautiful on the exterior. It was a two-story home in one of those neighborhoods where there were many other homes with the same color and style. I stretched my limbs as I got out of the truck while Charvo got the kids out of the car. Then, we all trailed behind him to the front door. He had the email with access instructions pulled up on his phone as he entered the access code.

The home layout was family-efficient, and I appreciated

the child safety features since our children were young. Even Kambrel, being the tallest of our bunch, couldn't reach the latch to open the back patio door, where a kidney-shaped pool awaited us.

"I want this room! It has Princess Tiana all over the walls," Taika gushed. Her eyes were wide with awe as she glanced over the decorated bedroom. It was truly fit for a princess.

Our boys settled on sharing a room, even though there were more than enough for everyone to sleep alone. Their room was Roblox-themed, with two twin beds on either side of the room. Walking away from their room, I heard them jumping on the beds and play-fighting, but I ignored them. We were finally on the perfect family vacation, and I wouldn't ruin it.

I made my way to the kitchen to start putting away the few items I brought along for this trip. I had preordered groceries from Walmart to be dropped off in a few hours, so we didn't have a reason to leave on our first day. Charvo was going fire up the grill while I made the sides, and the kids played in the pool—at least, that's what the plan was supposed to be.

"You like the house? Which room did you pick for us?" Since the home had three master suites, we could've chosen any of them for us to share.

"Whichever you choose is fine with me. The kids are sleeping upstairs." I smirked.

"Downstairs it is." We laughed.

"The groceries should be coming in a little bit. Do you want to check out the grill to see how it works? We don't have to do too much tonight. We can even do a pizza night if you don't feel like being out there."

"That's what I was coming to talk to you about. I need to go pick up a few things. Here, I'll leave you money to order whatever you want." Pulling his wallet out of his back pocket,

Charvo purposely ignored my glare because he knew I had a mouthful waiting for him. He set a thick wad of money on the kitchen counter before walking around, kissing me on the forehead, and walking out. I heard him open the front door, but then quick footsteps rapidly approached the kitchen. "Forgot the keys," he said, snatching them off the breakfast table.

Instead of waiting for his return, I got on the internet and ordered an early dinner for the kids and me. As we waited for the food, I watched them play in the pool and took videos and pictures from the side. When dinner arrived, we sat poolside and ate. Then, after waiting the standard fifteen minutes post-meal to avoid cramps, we were all in the pool, playing, racing, and splashing around.

The hours quickly ticked away as we found ourselves in the family movie room of the home with the chairs reclined and blankets keeping us warm as we snacked on popcorn, mom-made slushies, and candy. I wasn't sure what movie the kids had me watching; I was just happy to be in the moment with them.

"Mom..." I felt one of the kids tapping me and calling my name, and my eyes popped open.

"What happened, Kambrel?"

"Can we get cereal, or do you want us to wait for you to make breakfast?"

"Breakfast? What time is it? Did we fall asleep in here?" Looking around in confusion, I realized I was still in the recliner in the movie room.

"We did, but we were all comfortable, so I guess it's okay." He shrugged.

"Give me a minute, baby. I'll be out there in a few. Y'all can have some cereal for now, but don't overeat because I want to cook."

We were going to Disney today, so we needed to get up and

get together. I purchased advanced entry passes so we could get into the park an hour early.

Me: Why didn't you wake us up when you came in?

The kids sat quietly in the kitchen, Taika's tablet at the center of the table, while they watched Bluey.

"Waffles, sausage, and potatoes are fine?" I asked the kids, and they all nodded in agreement.

The Mickey Mouse waffle maker I brought from Target was the perfect touch for the mouse-shaped waffles. As I got all the food going, I rechecked my phone to see if Charvo responded. Not having a message from him, I made my way to the bedroom he chose for us, but when I opened the door and didn't see him, I was frozen. Figuring he probably changed his mind and wanted an upstairs room, I rushed up the stairs two at a time. Going room to room, my anger grew each time I closed the bedroom doors. Charvo wasn't here.

My anger bubbled to the surface as I marched down the stairs. I went to the kitchen to finish putting breakfast together as Charvo's absence nicked away at my mood.

"After we eat, I want y'all to clean yourselves up and put on the lotion I laid out on the bed before y'all put on the clothes." As a mother, I was often forced to suppress my true emotions so the kids couldn't tell that something was bothering me. How the fuck was this a family vacation, but the man of the house never made it back to be with us? This was strike one, and I feared the other two would be checked off before the sun fell tonight.

I was putting on my socks in the bedroom when I heard the front door open and shut. He tried to close it softly, but that was a wasted effort.

"I'm about to shower so we can leave." Charvo's voice entered the room before he physically did.

As soon as he opened and shut the bedroom door, my

sneakers met his face, followed by the bottle of lotion, perfume, and belt.

"You really got me fucked up if you think you're going anywhere with us. Where the fuck have you been, Charvo? This vacation was your idea, but you didn't even make it back last night." Pacing the floor, I was doing my best to keep myself from exploding the way I wanted to because I didn't want the kids to hear us arguing.

"I told you I had some stuff to pick up, baby, chill. I'm here now, and everything is all good with us. I was trying to make it back, but the time caught up with me. You and the kids have all my attention for the remainder of the trip. It was lingering business that needed to be handled before anything else. I'm sorry, Kaila. I swear that shit won't happen again."

"It shouldn't have happened in the first place!! You left us alone on a family fucking vacation. I should've listened to Pepper and kept my ass home."

"Man, if you keep listening to her, you'll find yourself lonely, just like her ass. House full of kids, but ain't no nigga out here trying to claim her ass," Charvo countered.

"Fuck you and fuck her. This was your opportunity to show up for the kids and me, but you're already fucking up. Just when I thought you could change and make shit better for us, you're fucking up."

"I'm sorry, Kaila, damn! I'm here now. I'm about to get dressed so we can go."

"The kids and I are going to my truck. If you aren't dressed by the time I crank up, you can take whatever bitch you were with last night to fucking Disney World."

"I wasn't with a—"

"Get out of my fucking way." I waved him off as I snatched my shoes off the floor and left the room.

I started loading the truck as the kids sat in the living

room, putting on their shoes. Once I finished, I used my selfie stick to take pictures of us. The kids were in positive moods and excited for Disney, so I knew they didn't hear the little spat between Charvo and me.

The truck cranked as the front door opened, but I quickly shifted to reverse and eased out of the driveway. Charvo was on the porch, shouting and raising his arms to gain my attention. My face remained unchanged while I died with laughter on the inside.

From the rearview mirror, I saw him run out of the yard and begin chasing the truck. "Mommy, look at Daddy!" Kambrel yelled before he started laughing.

"You forgot, Daddy, Mommy." Cadell snickered.

"I'm sorry, babies... I forgot him," I lied, slowing the truck down to give him time to catch up.

"Daddy, run faster!" Taika had her window down as she shouted at her dad.

Charvo was running for his life. Just as he got close to the truck, I inched up a bit, making him run a little further.

"Mommy almost forgot you," Cadell teased as Charvo got in the truck.

"I know, son. Ya mama crazy as hell." He panted, trying to catch his breath.

I sat in the driver's seat, laughing at his goofy ass. Charvo was shooting me the death glare as I focused on the LED monitor displaying the directions for us to get to Disney World.

"Hmm, you made it," I mumbled, only loud enough for him to hear me.

"You knew I was coming, Kaila. You childish for that."

"I thought you were down for the games." I smirked.

I was cranking up on his ass. Chavo had me fucked up if he

thought I was going to let him get away with that disappearing act on the first night.

"Before we get dirty, I want a picture in front of the castle," I told my family as I scanned the area for one of the Disney photographers.

"I want to go on the rides, Mommy," Taika pouted.

"Me too!" the boys said in unison.

"As soon as we take a picture with our best smiles, we can get on rides. Since we came early, we won't have to wait in long lines. I promise we can go as soon as we get a good picture."

The kids pouted but quickly fell into place once the photographer positioned us for the perfect photo in front of the castle.

"I know y'all aren't taking a picture without Auntie Pepper!" Hearing her voice, I looked around until my eyes landed on hers. She ran to me and hugged me as we screamed in excitement.

"Why the hell didn't you tell me you were coming?"

"I wanted to surprise my family, girl! Charvo's ass hit me up and asked if I could bring the kids."

"That's what I'm talking about. I guess he does have a damn brain." We laughed. "Come on, let's get some pictures so the kids can hit the rides before it gets crazy out here."

I noticed a quick exchange between Charvo and Pepperann that seemed more friendly than usual. Putting the two of them in a room was always like mixing lighter fluid and a damn match; it was almost guaranteed there would be a damn fire. I was thankful they set aside the petty shit for us to have a good vacation. Pepperann wasn't my blood sister, but we'd been running together since our playground days, so I wouldn't have had it any other way.

The kids enjoyed themselves with their cousins, and thanks to the fast passes and the early park admission, they got on every ride they desired without having to wait in long lines. As Pepper and I walked ahead with the kids to figure out what we wanted for lunch, I didn't notice Charvo falling back from the group and eventually disappearing altogether.

"That nigga ain't even come back to the house last night. He strolled in around 6:30 this morning, talking about he was handling business."

"The first night, Kaila?" Pepper was shocked.

All I could do was shake my head. It was embarrassing to speak on, but I needed to vent.

"He said he was handling business, but you know a woman's intuition doesn't lie. He was with a bitch last night. The only reason I didn't lose my shit was because of the kids. We haven't been on a vacation in three years, and they deserve this."

"And you deserve to be happy. I hope your ass isn't still considering fixing this shit. It's a mess and probably way too gone at this point."

"I know. I'm going to play the game for now. I have a place in mind that I can afford for now, so I'll make my move once we get back home. I can't believe it started on bullshit."

"All the nigga gives your ass is bullshit. Let him do what he has to do for the kids, and go find your husband, sis!"

"I know that's right," I agreed as we slapped hands.

We got the kids settled in to eat at The Crystal Palace, and Pepper excused herself to use the restroom. I had each of the kids line up for us to wash our hands at a sink near the restrooms before giving them each a plate to go through the buffet.

My eyes scanned the restaurant in search of Pepper. She was coming from the restrooms, and a few seconds later, Charvo emerged from the same area with a big bouquet of red roses and a small ring box in hand.

CHAPTER SIX
CHARVO HARRIS

I knew Kaila would be pissed that I had to leave as soon as we got to the house, but she had no choice but to understand a nigga had to make a play. My phone was on 'Do Not Disturb' as I drove up to Orlando, but when I finally checked it, I had hella missed calls and texts from Alexia and Green. Alexia had been trailing us from Miami, but her ass was driving so stupid on the highway I had to pull over at the rest stop to tell her to get her shit together before she blew my spot.

Alexia and I had made many plays together. She was a woman about her business and only focused on getting to a bag, so there were never any romantic lines crossed, even though she hinted at wanting more from me at times.

The hotel I put her in for the night was just outside the gated community where Kaila and I were staying with the kids. I needed her nearby, so if some shit popped off or went sideways, I'd be able to pull up and regulate if need be.

Alexia was sitting in the back of her car, puffing one of those fruity ass vapes as she awaited my arrival.

"I just got checked in, nigga. I thought I'd at least have a night to chill before we got to work. I did want to get some shopping done at the outlets," Alexia said as I approached.

"And I thought I could chill with my ol' lady and kids, but here I am with you," I countered. "Green is ready to make the play. You got the cash?"

She pointed over her shoulder, signaling that the money was inside the car. "All five-dollar bills," she remarked.

Green was particular about how he accepted payments. Sometimes, he wanted singles, and other times, he requested big bills. When he called the shots, I did as instructed. Although there wasn't a nigga on this earth who I feared, when it came to stacking my own bread, I wasn't making the wrong moves.

"Aight, it's at the spot in Malibu Groves. In and out, Alexia. He said it's ready, and it'll be a clean exchange. We ain't got time for your bullshit tonight."

"What about your bullshit?"

"Man, let's go."

Laughing at my response, she took one more puff from her vape before jumping off her trunk. I waited for Alexia to pull out of the parking lot before taking another route to our destination. I wanted to be extra cautious in case Green had someone on our trail. He was a sneaky ass nigga, so I liked to remain a few steps ahead of him at all times.

I knew Alexia's ass was on some dumb shit when I made it to the spot before her. Knowing her, she probably made a damn stop along the way. Instead of waiting for her, I parked the Suburban near the curb and went inside to chop it up with Green before we got down to business.

"Man, yo' mama been on my ass since that shit went down. You need to tell her to chill. We got everything under control." Green started talking shit as soon as he opened the door and dapped me up.

"They shot up yo' mama's shit, nigga. Ain't nothing under control." I chuckled.

"That shit ain't have nothing to do with me. The niggas I hit still clueless as fuck. Trust me, I know them niggas don't know what hit them."

"And how you figure that?" I asked, curious to know his answer.

"Them niggas post everything on social media. If they were looking for me, my face would've been plastered all over the Gram. Trust me, everything is cool," he spoke reassuringly.

"I hear you." I nodded. "Lex is supposed to be pulling up. Her crazy ass probably stopped at the fucking store or some shit, but she got the bread."

"How the fuck you pull that one off? You doing the family shit with hella bitches on your team making plays for you. That's the type of time I'm trying to be on. She got a sister or something?"

"Nigga, shut yo ass up! No, I ain't got no damn sister. It's only me, and you're too wishy-washy for me." Alexia didn't bother tapping on the door before she barged in, eavesdropping on our conversation. She had a red hot sausage in a small plastic bag with a bag of salt and vinegar chips and a peach Ritz soda. I gave her a stern look when she made eye contact, but she brushed me off. Her ass knew that store run wasn't a part of the plan.

"If you weren't playing games, I would've snatched you up long ago." Green winked, and she fake gagged.

"Where yo' other niggas at? Specifically, the one who was here last time. Light-skinned one with the low fade? Now that motherfucker could get it," Alexia inquired.

"See, yo' ass worried about the wrong shit now. Where's the bread?"

"I'm not counting that shit again, so take it or leave it," Alexia said as the travel bag hit the ground with a loud thud.

My phone vibrated in my back pocket, which surprised me. I didn't remember switching it off 'Do not Disturb.'

"I need to take this," I told them as I reached for the doorknob.

Before I pressed the phone to my ear, I could hear her on the other end talking shit.

"Where you at, Charvo? This lady is saying they don't take this kind of card, so I can't check in."

"I'm busy right now. Give me an hour or so, and I'll be there."

"An hour won't work. We're all tired and hungry. This is exactly why I should've stayed my ass the fuck home. You already brought that bitch and her kids. I should've known you wouldn't have time for us."

"Who said I won't have time? I'm in the middle of something. Give me some time, you hear me?"

"Just send the money to my other account so I can check in. I just told you we're hungry."

"Look, go get something to eat with them. As soon as I'm finished over here, I'll be there. Yo ass needs to get a real fucking bank account and let that Cashapp shit go."

"Fuck you. Everybody else takes my card. You're the one who picked this high-class hotel. They think they too good for my money or some shit."

"We'll get it worked out when I pull up. Feed them kids and keep that shit tight for me," I flirted before ending the call.

I made my way back inside the house and paused when I noticed how silent it had become. Usually, Alexia and Green couldn't stop getting on each other's nerves, so it was out of place for them to be silent.

"Yoo," I called out, trying to signal them that I was coming just in case they found themselves in a compromising position.

I walked to the back den and turned a corner, walking right up to a scene my mind struggled to process. Green was laid out on the carpeted floor with a knife sticking out the side of his neck. His eyes rolled in the back of his head, and I could hear him gargling as he struggled to breathe.

"What the fuck?" I was stunned.

"Get the fucking shit, and let's go, Charvo! Why are you standing there looking stupid?" Alexia walked out of a bedroom carrying three duffle bags that looked too heavy for her petite frame.

"What the fuck is going on right now, Lex? You need to start talking. We are not making another move until you tell me what the fuck type of time you're on."

"What else is there to explain? Your cousin is a weird-ass, grimy-ass nigga. I got his ass before he could get us." Alexia dropped her bags, reached down, and snatched a pistol from his waistband. "You think that's just for decoration? His mom's house got shot up, and he's acting like that shit doesn't faze him. His mama, Charvo! This is the type of nigga a snake wouldn't even trust. Now, are you going to help me, or do I need to lay you the fuck out too?" She still had a firm grip on the gun, but I quickly snatched that shit away from her. Knowing her crazy ass, she would put a hot one in my ass without a second thought.

"That's what the fuck I thought." Alexia picked up the bags and proceeded to the front door.

Giving my blood cousin one last look, all I could do was step over him to get the product and the money. There were bags full of drugs and money that we loaded into Alexia's car with quickness.

"I need you to return to Miami tonight, Lex."

"Tonight?" She challenged and turned to face me as we walked out of the bedroom, carrying the last few bags.

"Look, shit finna get real hot, and you know I don't want you caught up in none of this. Can you do this, please, without arguing?"

Rolling her eyes, she eventually agreed.

Outside the house, Lex passed me the travel bag she had given to Green upon her arrival. "Take care of the wifey and kids this weekend. It is a pleasure doing business, as always. I'll hit you when I touch down."

"See, that's the Alexia I love right there. You're the one, not the two, girl. Get your ass out of here now, though! No speeding or driving like you just got in this damn country. You hear me?"

She shot me a bird before getting in her car and peeling out of the driveway.

Before I left, I quickly wiped the house clean of our prints and killed all the lights on my way out. I was sure Green would be found eventually; I just prayed shit didn't heat up until this family vacation ended.

Arriving at the Disney resort, I parked in a handicapped spot before heading inside to figure out the hotel arrangements for Shawty. I knew our situation was unconventional, but I also wanted to show her how much I appreciated what she did for me. When she came over to the house the other night, she really could've put a nigga on blast for letting her rest her head over there, but she kept her mouth closed. I had always been the kind of nigga to reward good behavior, so for that, it was only right that I treated her and her jits to an all-expenses paid Disney vacation, allowing me to kill two birds with one stone.

I presented my American Express card to the woman at the main desk and was able to resolve everything by the time she returned to the hotel with the kids. I could tell they were exhausted, so I stepped in and assisted her with preparing them for bed. The two-bedroom suite provided us privacy once we got the kids situated.

"I'm only chilling for a bit, and then I've got to get back to Kaila and the kids."

"Ughh—must you say her name in my presence? You know I don't like hearing that."

"Bring yo' ass over here and bend the fuck over."

"Can we at least have a drink first? I'm trying to loosen up and not rush through this. I won't spend much time with you this weekend, so I want to make the most of it." She walked up to me and wrapped her arms around my neck before reaching up to kiss me.

"Yeah. I need something on my stomach, though. I've been on go all day. Driving up here, getting them situated, then I had to handle some shit with my people. I'm hungry, horny, and tired as hell."

"I got all that, baby. Get comfortable in the bed, and I'll be right back."

After she pecked my lips again, I did as instructed, kicking my shoes off and getting comfy in the king-sized bed.

She brought in a steak with mashed potatoes and broccoli on a plate. I knew she hadn't cooked it; she must've grabbed me something while out with the kids. I appreciated her effort.

While devouring the meal, shawty had my dick in her mouth, taking her time to please me as I filled my growling stomach. Every time I felt her slide it further down her throat, I had to move the plate to get a good look at her. She knew how to work that motherfuckin dick; that was precisely why I wasn't coming up off her ass.

She had my shit brick hard by the time I finished eating, and I was ready to fuck. Baby grabbed my plate and left the room before returning with two glasses of brown liquor.

"I want you to fuck me all night, Daddy. Can you do that for me?" Tapping her glass against mine, she downed the drink without flinching.

"You know I gotta go, but let's make the best of this." Following her lead, I tipped the glass, and the liquid rushed down my throat. As I took one last gulp, I stared at the bottom of the glass, noticing a white residue staring back at me.

"I meant *all night*." That was the last thing I heard before I felt my body collapse.

My head pounded as I awoke in the most uncomfortable position. I tried to move but realized I was on the floor and had the weight of my body on one arm while my neck was twisted in a different direction.

"Fuck," I groaned in pain as I slowly eased myself from the floor. The room was spinning as I managed to get myself in a seated position on the side of the bed.

I heard her watching a video on her phone and laughing every few seconds like she was at a fucking comedy show.

"What time is it, man? This is exactly why I don't take this shit to the next level with you. How the fuck I'm supposed to be yo' nigga, but you lacing my shit?"

"Ain't nobody did nothing to you, Charvo. Calm all that shit down before you wake up the kids."

"Fuck you and them fucking kids, bitch! I told you I gotta go. I don't even feel like I can drive right now."

"You better figure out what you're doing because I'm about to get them up and ready to head to the park," she spat.

"Ready for the park?"

"It's almost six in the morning. I want to get there early."

"Fuck, man!! Fuck!" I raged. I pulled myself upright and

took unsteady steps to the restroom to relieve my aching bladder.

She was out of the bedroom when I emerged again, which was a good move on her part because I was ready to lay hands on her stupid ass. This wasn't the first time she'd hit a nigga with a knockout combo that had me begging and pleading with Kaila to forgive me for my bullshit. She knew her role, but jealousy sometimes arose, leaving me caught up.

I was still feeling out of my body as I walked around Disney World, trying to hold my shit together. I honestly expected Kaila to be gone with the kids since the sun beat me back home. Her being there let me know there was still a chance for us. I wanted nothing more than to spend the rest of my life with her and the kids, and I prayed she didn't pie a nigga when I did propose. I couldn't say I was man enough to take that.

Pepper had an attitude when she met me outside the restaurant and gave me the ring box. I had custom flowers delivered there late last night, so they were at the concierge desk, waiting for me to pick them up. We coordinated the proposal together because I knew I needed her on my side to help me get back into Kaila's good graces.

"She sitting down?" I asked. I knew the nervousness I felt was evident.

"Yeah, she ready. I told her I was going to the bathroom."

"You walk in first, and I'm right behind you."

"You better get this shit right, Charvo. I don't appreciate being sent to Walmart to make this shit happen."

"Why the fuck you so loud, damn?" My eyes widened.

"I'm just honest. Yo' ass better have her replacement

coming soon or else, fuck nigga," she said before heading back into the restroom.

I spotted Kaila before she saw me. Initially, she wore a scowl, but her face softened when she noticed the flowers. As I approached, Pepper had her phone up, recording the moment because I knew Kaila would want to hold onto this one forever.

"Kaila, I know I haven't been the perfect man, but I'm here today to tell you that I've laid that young boy to rest, and I'm on bended knee as the man you need me to be. I want forever with you and our kids. I promise to love and see you through the good and bad times. I promise to honor and cherish you. I promise to be the best father I can be to our children and hopefully get one or two more out of you." Getting down on one knee, I opened the ring box, and my heart dropped to my asshole when I only saw the Walmart price tag inside the box but no ring.

My eyes shot over to Pepper, and she was laughing at my expense.

Kaila stepped forward and grabbed the ring box out of my hand. The price tag read in bright red numbers, $79.99.

"Charvo—"

"Did you really think I was going to let the nigga we've been sharing propose to you, sis?" Pepperann laughed menacingly.

She started a slow clap as Kaila stared between her and me. I couldn't hear what she was saying, but I saw her mouth start moving. I was too focused on trying to get my hands around Ann's neck for ruining our moment.

"Sharing, Charvo?? I'm about to kill you and that bitch!" Kaila tossed the box in my face and tried to lunge at me, but a random man in the crowd got between us.

With angry tears streaming down her face, Kaila abruptly started gathering our kids and their belongings. A small crowd formed around us to watch the spectacle. Even though I was begging her to listen, she wasn't trying to hear anything I had to say. Suddenly, Pepperann was nowhere in sight, but our kids remained at the table.

"If I ever see you again, you better make sure your mama has her black dress ready, fuck nigga!" Kaila spat before storming past me with our kids in tow.

Frantically searching the restaurant for Pepperann, I felt my phone vibrate in my pocket with a message notification.

Ann: Since you never wanted to choose, I made the decision for you. See you soon, baby daddy. Muah!!

CHAPTER SEVEN

TYREE ROMAN

"I don't give a fuck if they got Mickey Mouse in the whip with them. As soon as they pull away from that shit, lay everybody down! I just jumped on I-4. When I get over there, I better see a big white Suburban on the side of the road." I ended the call and pressed down on the gas a little harder to make it to Disney World.

We touched down in the O last night, ready to knock that nigga Green off, but to our surprise, we were beaten to the punch. The nigga was clinging to life when Keem got to him, and I told him to call the doc to keep his ass alive. We needed to know who ran through his shit with our product and money, so if he thought he was taking the coward's way out, he was wrong.

Doc and the team worked on Green's ass for close to four hours. He wasn't all the way right, and truthfully, he'd never be, but he was okay enough for us to keep him around for a few more days. Keem and I rounded up the top shooters to complete this quickly and efficiently.

The drop on a white Suburban came from Keem's top

shooter, sitting in the empty house across from Green's spot. He was ready to go in with guns blazing to lay everybody out, but I didn't green light that shit. I wanted to lay eyes on the sheisty-ass motherfuckers. I needed to look into the eyes of the nigga who thought his balls were bigger than mine. While running the streets, I didn't have a single soul brave enough to see what type of time I was on. Now that Keem was at the head of the table, niggas were getting at him left and right. I knew he could handle it, but the fact that I was in Orlando to help clean up his mess had me second-guessing my decision.

J Way was hitting my line again, so I assumed it was an update on the Suburban. Since I was two blocks from his current location, I didn't answer the call.

Arriving on the scene, I saw J Way attempting to calm a woman who remained planted on the metal step attached to the side of the truck. I parked behind her truck and got out of mine. Approaching them, I could tell by her puffy, red, and swollen eyes that she had been crying. I prayed this nigga ain't do anything off the wall.

"Ain't nobody in this fucking truck but me and my kids! If I have to tell you again, I swear on my fucking kids, I'm going to get out of my truck and beat your fucking ass." She attempted to slam the door shut, but J Way's leg was blocking her from closing it all the way. Reaching out of the truck, she yanked him by his shirt into the truck and then shoved him back out. I heard the loud zap before J Way let out a loud groan, and his body hit the ground, twitching. The buzzing noise didn't stop as she opened her door and stepped down. "You came to fuck with me, right? Is this what you wanted? Come on, nigga! I got something that'll light your ass up like a Christmas tree. Come on!! Get your weak ass up," she commanded as she tapped the button to ignite the taser once more.

Physically, she was a mess. Her tear-stained face had

quickly transformed into the face of a woman filled with rage. A few bright red locs atop her head spilled out of the messy bun, and her custom Disney t-shirt was disheveled. She had to be around 5'8" because she wasn't far from my 6'1" frame. I wasn't the best at guessing a woman's weight because my mom raised me to love and accept all women, but she had endless curves that were a sight for sore eyes.

"Come on now, sweetheart. Put the taser down. My partner was trying to talk to you." I spoke calmly, keeping my hands by my sides so I wouldn't startle her.

"I already told him I don't know who Green is, and if you're looking for my baby daddy, he's not with me. I don't know what he got himself caught up in, but my kids and I just left Disney World. I suggest you step back so I can leave. You're fine as hell, but I won't hesitate to light your ass up, too," she warned, tapping the button on the taser for a quick spark.

"We can talk without the weapon. What's your baby daddy's name, mama?"

"Why do you need to know that? What he does has nothing to do with me and my kids," she quizzed.

"He was spotted in this truck on the wrong side of the city yesterday. If you tell me where he is, I can let you go. I apologize if J Way was a bit aggressive... that's what we do. Do you know where he is right now?"

"Most likely still at the fucking park with his bitch..." Silent tears slipped down her face.

I never liked for a woman to look me in the face while she cried. Although I knew her emotions had nothing to do with me, that shit still made me feel bad. I never knew what to say or do in those situations, so I just stood there like a damn fool, watching her.

"Can I leave now? I already made myself look foolish. I have a lot going on right now, and I really can't take on anything else. It's only me and my kids in the truck. I wouldn't lie to protect that fuck nigga."

"How does he know Green?" I deadpanned, not acknowledging her attempts to leave.

"I just told you I don't know who the fuck Green is."

"Is this how you talk to your daddy?"

"Don't worry about how the fuck I talk to my dad, nigga. I'm on the side of an isolated road, my kids are asleep inside the truck, and two strange men are questioning me. If I'm hostile, y'all and that fuck nigga Charvo are the reason for it. Now, this is my last time asking before I do you how I did him." She glanced down at J Way, who was still lying on the ground with his eyes wide open. The nigga was still breathing, but I knew he was reeling from being tased. That little powerful shit she had was police grade, so I knew he was tweaking out.

"I'm going to reach into my pocket for my phone. Can you not—" I pointed at the taser, but she hit the button on the side to light it up. I wasn't in the mood to be tweaked the fuck out for the rest of the day after getting shocked by that shit.

"Hurry up before my kids wake up," she stressed.

I grabbed my phone and went to the message thread between Keem and me. The last few pictures he sent me were of Green, and a few of them included his people. I set my phone down on the road and stepped back, allowing her the space and opportunity to freely pick it up.

"I need you to look through those pictures and tell me if you recognize anyone. The person we're looking for was last seen in this truck. I'm trying to put the pieces together to send you on your way."

"My baby daddy had the truck all night. He didn't make it back in until 6:30 this morning. I wouldn't be surprised if he was—" She was absent-mindedly speaking when her voice trailed off. "This my baby daddy. Which one is Green?"

"The fat one in the middle." She zoomed in on the photo to get a better look.

"That's the nigga with the old ass name. It's Gerald, I think. They're cousins. I don't know what Charvo got himself caught up in with that nigga; both of them move funny as fuck. Charvo knows not to even bring him around my kids. Is that all you need from me?"

"As much as I want to, I can't let you leave like that. I need to pick your brain a little more. Your baby daddy got himself caught up in some hot shit, and I'm trying to get to the bottom of it."

"And how do I know you aren't lying to me about all of this?"

"There is a tan bag in your truck under the spare tire. It could be full of drugs, money, or a combination of both. How much do you think your bond will be if you get pulled over with that?"

"See, now I know you're full of shit. I loaded my trunk myself this morning, and there was nothing extra. Before I lose my shit on you, I suggest you let me leave."

"Pop the trunk, and let's check it out. I'm almost positive you didn't check underneath that tire."

"And if you're wrong, I'm leaving. I must return to the vacation house and get our stuff. I don't want to run into him while we are there." I saw a flash of fear in her eyes when she spoke.

"That nigga put hands on you?" I raised an eyebrow. Fuck whatever else we were talking about.

She passed my phone back to me, quickly turned around, and returned to the truck to engage the trunk release. As it slowly lifted, I waited for her to come back around before I approached. I didn't know if she was going to try to shock my ass, and I wasn't trying to find out.

As she waited for the trunk to rise completely, I scanned the exposed parts of her body from head to toe. There weren't any physical bruises that I could see, but with the makeup and shit these women knew how to use, ain't no telling.

"See, besides what I packed in here today, it's nothing extra. She moved the packed bags for their day trip to Disney out of the way. There were snacks, juices, clothes, and shoes; more than enough for one day at that expensive ass park.

"Lift that latch right there." I pointed to the release flap.

She struggled to open it, so I warned her that I was approaching to assist. She looked at me suspiciously but stepped aside so I could do it. The spare tire and the tan bag were stuffed tightly inside the small space, so removing the cover piece took a little muscle. Her eyes widened at the sight of the tan bag; her shock was genuine.

"I don't know how that got in there or what's even in there," she stammered.

"I know you don't. That said, I need you to follow me back to my hotel." I swiped the taser out of her loose grip while she was distracted.

"Give me that back. I won't use it on you." She spoke in an irritated tone as she held her hand out for me to give it to her.

"I'll give it back once we make it to my hotel. I need you to get in a clear mental space for a little minute. I know I'm coming at you with a lot, and you don't know me from a grain of salt, but I promise you, I'm only doing what I can to look out for the wellbeing of you and your jits."

"Let me see what's in that bag." She reached for the tan bag, but I quickly snatched it away.

"Nah, I doubt you want to know what's in here." Based on the weight of the bag, I knew it was at least a few bricks, a gun, and possibly cash. She didn't need to know what was in there.

"Just open it and let me peek. I'll happily follow you wherever you want to go." A sly smile appeared as we locked eyes.

Against my better judgment, I allowed her to take a peek inside the bag, and sitting right at the top was a pistol.

"Fuck..." I mumbled before she exploded.

"It's always me! Always the one who has to suffer the consequences of a fuck nigga's actions! My kids and I have nothing to do with whatever Charvo has going on. All I wanted was a nice family vacation to fucking Disney and for the nigga to give me the proper proposal I deserve. You know what I got in return?" She paused as if she expected me to answer her question. "The nigga pied me... and on top of all that, he had a fucking ring box from Walmart with no ring in it."

I had yet to fully understand a woman's strength. The fact that she had completely broken down in front of me yet again may have been a sign of weakness to some, but it was far from that. This woman held the world on her shoulders and was most likely holding down the kids on her own, on top of dealing with everything her baby daddy threw at her.

This time, when she cried, I took the risk of pulling her into my embrace. She cried into my chest without holding back. The silence between us was comfortable; I hadn't even shared a moment like this with either of my children's mothers, and I loved them both dearly.

J Way's stirring on the ground interrupted us, and she stepped away from me. He stood slowly with his eyes fixed on the woman. "The bitch is crazy as hell! I don't know what type of fucking stun gun that is, but she needs to be locked up for that lethal shit. I swear my ass just died and came back," he fumed.

"J, take off in my whip. I got this," I told him.

Since he had been riding in a car with one of the other shooters who had already taken off, I figured that was the best way to get him away from the scene without causing further disruption. The original plan was for him to take off in the truck with the nigga we were looking for, but there was an immediate and necessary change of plans.

"You sure? I don't want her to light you up, nigga. Shit will stop your heart three times," J Way warned, and shawty laughed.

"I told you not to fuck with me." She shrugged, wiping away the last of her tears.

"I'm good. She about to drop me off," I winked as her head whipped back in my direction. I tossed J Way the keys and then refocused my attention on her. "You ready?"

"You better get in the car with him before he pulls off. I'm uncomfortable with a strange man getting in a vehicle with me and my children."

"Strange man? We've been talking for at least ten minutes."

"And you're still strange to me. I don't know your name or anything else about you."

"It's Tyree Roman, born and raised in Dade County. My parents are Latonya and Nixon Roman. They've been married for forty-something years. I have a big sister, Tomeka, and a little sister, Nayla. I have two children of my own, two baby mamas, and before you start thinking my shit is like the typical drama-filled setup, it's not. I like my life to be very organized. Almost everything I do is planned, every component of it."

"It sounds like you need a new assistant or something. I don't think this is going how you planned it." She laughed.

"Oh, it is... trust me, it's going exactly as I planned." Stepping around her, I headed for the driver's seat, thankful she hadn't locked the door and the truck was still running. "Are you coming with us? I don't want to wake up the sleeping children." I spoke to her through the window I'd let down.

"This is a brand-new truck—"

Shifting the truck to drive, I was about to lift my foot off the brake and leave her ass on the side of the road. I knew how to care for kids, so I wasn't sweating that part. She gave me a blank stare before walking around the truck and entering the passenger seat.

"If you do something to me and my kids, I got more than that little taser." She reached forward and tapped the glove compartment, which caused me to smirk. I liked a woman who knew how to protect herself.

As I inched away and merged into the smooth flow of traffic, she kept her eyes on me as if she were studying me. I planted a smile as I focused on the road. Once she took her eyes off me and pulled her phone out, she relaxed in the passenger seat. I quickly glanced over and noticed it was powering back on.

"How were you trying to get back to your hotel if your phone was off? That's unsafe as hell. What if some crazy ass nigga had you pulled over on the side of the road?"

"What if," she chuckled. "I'm about to give you the address, or do you want me to connect to my CarPlay?"

"I want you to sit back, relax, and tell me about yourself. You still haven't answered my earlier question, so let's start there. Is the nigga putting hands on you or not?" The uncomfortable stir in her seat and repositioning of her body answered the question, but I needed to hear it from her.

"I work at a nonprofit in Downtown Miami. I was born and raised in Broward but moved to Dade because of my kids' father. Both of my parents passed when I was too young to remember them, so my godmother raised me, and these are my three children."

"Name?"

"S—Samantha," she hesitated.

"Your name ain't no damn Samantha, I know that much."
We both laughed.

"It's Kaila, but you probably already knew that."

I purposely took my time getting to the hotel, hoping she'd fall asleep, but after a while, I was sure she realized I was going in circles.

Instead of taking them to the address she entered on the truck's GPS, I drove us to my hotel. When she was ready to be honest about her baby daddy, I'd let her get her shit. Until then, she and the kids would remain under my watchful eye. We also needed to have her nigga under our thumb to see how he would move next, so all this shit was sitting on ice for a minute.

"Tyree—"

"You still didn't answer the question. I need to know that you and the kids are safe."

"What's going on that would have us unsafe?"

"We found his cousin with a knife in his throat, and he most likely did that shit. Your man is moving like he's invincible, and I don't need that to change any time soon. If a man can attempt to kill his own family, ain't no telling his state of mind. Now that I've let you cry on my shoulder, you're stuck with me until we figure it out. I promise not to put you in harm's way as long as you listen to me."

She silently nodded her understanding. "Let me wake the kids up. All they need to know is that you're my friend."

As gently as a mother could, she woke each child and started getting them out of the truck. I made my presence known, and the kids were so tired that I didn't think it mattered who I was at the moment.

I picked up her youngest while she managed to get her oldest two to navigate themselves into the elevators and to my suite on a private floor. This floor was only accessible with a specific key card, of which I owned one of four copies. Two of them were given to each of my children's moms, and the general manager kept the fourth copy just in case.

As she stepped past me to exit the elevator, Kaila eyed me and walked directly into the suite.

"This is cute." She smirked, glancing around the space. Although her words downplayed it, I could tell she was amazed by the glimmer in her eyes.

"Who is that?" Her daughter sized me as she stood behind her mom.

"A friend, Taika." She forced a smile, which helped ease her children's worry. "We have to stay here for a few hours. Can we —" She looked around, signaling to me that she needed a moment with the kids.

I led the way to one of the four bedrooms in the suite that was made for kids. Whenever my children's mothers wanted to take a vacation with the kids, this suite was designed with them in mind. It was a split floor plan with two identical master suites on opposite sides.

I double-checked to make sure she didn't need anything else before I headed to the bedroom. I tapped the FaceTime icon beside Starja's name as I took a seat on the sofa.

"It's funny that you don't answer when I call, but if I would've missed this call, you would've sent the damn SWAT team over here to kick down my door."

"You damn right. Answer this motherfucker when I call." We laughed. "I need you to do me a favor and get in touch with Vanessa too. I want the kids in Orlando tomorrow."

"What's the favor?"

"A background check."

CHAPTER EIGHT
CHARVO HARRIS

"You are always ready to up and leave when your boys call you to go sit outside the fucking corner store, but when I ask you to spend time with us, it's a problem. It's Kambrel's birthday, Charvo. Are you really going to leave and not spend today with us?" Kaila was whining nonstop as I maneuvered through our bedroom to get dressed.

Green had hit my line, saying he needed me to hold one of his spots down for a few hours. Kaila would have to understand that a nigga had to hustle to take care of them. All this bullshit could wait.

"Kaila, he's turning two. He won't even remember this fucking party. I told you I didn't want him to have one anyway. Yo' hard-headed ass could've got some cake and ice cream and left it at that."

"You promised me that we would do better when it came to putting time into our family, Charvo! Your ass was barely there for Taika, and now you're walking out on Kambrel's birthday, and you act like you don't even want to be around Cadell the majority of the time. I swear, my biggest regret is meeting you. I don't regret my kids, but I swear to God, if they could've gotten another parent, a man who actually wants to take care of them, I wouldn't be in this damn predicament."

I knew she was saying shit to push my buttons, but I was doing my best to let it roll off my back. I had places to be and money to make. I wasn't in the mood to fight with her because I needed a clear head while handling business today.

"Look, when I make it back home tonight, I'll have a gift for the nigga. That's the least I can do. I go above and beyond to show you and them that I love y'all, but I swear to God you do and say dumb shit to push a nigga away. It's only so much I can take."

"If you feel like I'm doing too much because I want me and my kids to come first in your life, then you can pack all your shit up and keep it moving. I should've listened to my friends and let your broke ass go a long time ago."

Launching across the room, I had her ass pressed against the wall with her feet dangling beneath her as I menacingly stared into her eyes.

"You keep listening to what them hoes talking about, and you gon' end up just like them! All them niggas do is fuck for the hot forty dollars and send them on their way. Do you want to be a hoe, Kaila? Is that what the fuck you want? Since you want to be like her so fucking bad, drop my kids off at my mama's house and go on about your business. I ain't got time for the mother of my kids to be out here on some dumb shit to try to prove a point to me. I keep telling you the people you hang with are bad influences on you and our kids, but you refuse to hear me out. With that said, do what the fuck you got to do, bitch!! I'm sick of your shit." I repeatedly slammed her into the wall as she screamed and tried to fight back, but my grip on her arms was too tight.

Since she had gained almost a hundred pounds after having Cadell, her weight had my arms trembling, so I couldn't do anything but let her fat ass hit the ground.

Kaila was crying, and when I turned around, our daughter

Taika was standing in the doorway, crying as she watched the commotion. I grabbed my Nike slides and walked toward the door. I went to kiss my daughter, but she jumped back away from me.

"It's okay, Taika. Mommy's okay. Come here," Kaila coaxed.

"You know I love you and Mommy, baby girl. Daddy didn't mean any of that." I bent down on one knee to be at eye level with my daughter. "Come here and give me a hug." She took a big gulp as she looked between me and her mom. I thought she was going to come to me, but she ran past me to get to her mom.

Kaila's snake ass was trying to turn my kids against me. I could feel that shit in my bones. I didn't even notice the decorations Kaila had around the house as I made my way to the front door. She knew I didn't even like people knowing where we laid our heads, so this whole party situation was blowing the fuck out of me. I smacked one of the balloons down, causing it to pop as I rounded a corner. My sons were in the living room watching some baby ass show on the television. Shaking my head at them, I threw up the deuces as I walked out of the apartment.

Green was standing outside his car waiting when I pulled up to Fuel Stop Express. He pressed one phone against his ear with another in his hand as he paced. There were two other niggas out there with him as if they were his security. Although he was my blood cousin, I hated the way this nigga moved. He desperately wanted to be the king of Miami, but his character wouldn't allow him to move up further in the ranks. He was always about getting to his next dollar and stepping over anyone who got in the way. Green didn't give a fuck about burning bridges or keeping his face clean in the streets.

"What took you so long, nigga? Yo' ass done missed out on serving quite a few fiends already. I gotta take that shit off the top." He spoke to me as I approached to dap him up.

"Off the top? You know Kaila's ass was tripping about me leaving when it's one of my jits birthday today."

"*That shit ain't got nothing to do with my operation. Can you do this or not? I don't like incompetent motherfuckers.*"

"*I got it, Green. Pipe down with all that.*" *I waved him off.*

"*It's hot out here, too, so keep your eyes open.*" *Green signaled one of his security guards to pass the work to me, but I had him put it in my trunk. The last thing I needed was a young nigga to run down on me while I was out there and snatching everything I had.*

I waited about twenty minutes after Green left to get some snacks inside the gas station. My stomach had been growling since I had left the house without eating what Kaila had cooked, and I knew it was going to be a long day.

"*I keep telling these girls to stop dancing at the pumps!*" *I heard the complaining from behind the checkout counter. I followed his line of vision out the oversized window and saw a group of girls by pump six. Two of them were shaking ass for the other girl holding her phone up to record while another one stood at the pump to pay for their gas.* "*They always come up here broke, begging, and trying to steal,*" *he complained.*

I squinted to get a better view, but I couldn't tell if I recognized any of them or not. "*Let me go outside and talk to them real quick,*" *I told the clerk before exiting the gas station.*

Their music was blasting through the speakers of the small Honda. The car rattled as if it were ready to fall apart at a small gust of wind.

"*Why y'all out here making all this noise? Y'all stressing that man out with all this motion.*" *I didn't take my eyes away from the women who were still on top of the car, popping their asses to the beat of the music.*

"*Who the fuck is this nigga?*" *They all looked in my direction, and I locked my eyes on the one I recognized. I remembered seeing her at the house with Kaila a few times in the past.*

"*He ain't nobody in-damn-portant.*" *She rolled her eyes.*

"Damn, I was just coming out here to tell y'all to chill all that shit out. I'm not trying to be the bad guy."

"You coming out here trying to regulate like this your shit. You can go on about your business, Charvo. I'd hate to have to call Kaila and tell her you out here being too friendly."

"Why do we have to take it there, shawty? You putting my business out there and shit like I did something to you." The sly expression that appeared on her face let me know her ass was plotting.

"You did do something to me." She seductively licked her lips as she stared into my soul.

"And what might that be?"

"Shut yo' ass up and take this dick," I gritted. "Talking all that big shit, but you running from the dick." Looking down, I watched as my dick slid in and out of her unprotected. Although her pussy was on the looser side, it was wet and warm, just how I liked it.

The bathroom inside the gas station didn't provide much room for us to really go at it how I wanted to, but for the time being, we had to make it work.

I could tell she was struggling to take all ten inches as her whimpers became louder and her body squeamish, but I needed her to feel all of me. I slid inside her as deep as I could go, and she released a loud moan.

"Why you fucking me like this?"

"You must've forgotten you were talking shit to me like I owed you something, so I'm paying my dues." With a hard smack to the ass, I gripped her hair and yanked her neck back into my chest. Looking down into her eyes as I fucked her had my shit ready to spit up.

"Let me suck that cum, big daddy," she moaned into my ear.

I almost threw her ass into the wall as she maneuvered off me and dropped to her knees to catch my nut.

Tears streamed down her face as her nasty ass swallowed my dick whole.

I took a minute to wipe my shit off and tuck it back into my pants as she cleaned herself up.

"I hope yo' ass ain't got shit I can take home to my girl."

"Nigga, you better hope you ain't got shit that's gonna have me in the damn clinic."

"I'm straight. My bitch just went to the doctor a few weeks ago, so I know I'm good."

"The way you niggas think is going to have all of us dead out here." She shook her head as she reached for the doorknob.

"Aye, lock my number in so we can run this back when my bitch be tripping with the pussy."

She reached for my phone, and I gladly handed it to her. She saved her number under the name Pretty Pussy Ann, but I quickly changed that shit. I didn't need Kaila going through my shit and catching me slipping.

"I'll holla at you, Ann. Hold that shit tight for a nigga. I'm sure I'll be back through soon.

"Why the fuck do you go out of your way to make my life so miserable? I knew it was a mistake fucking with you. I should've left your bald-headed ass alone that night at the fucking gas station. What type of bitches talk to a nigga at the gas station anyway? You are a bottom feeder, shawty... I fucking hate you!"

Pepperann stood in my face, laughing at me as I cursed her out. I knew that eventually I'd get caught up fucking with her behind Kaila's back, but I didn't think it would go down like that. I literally had her hoe ass on my fucking payroll to keep her mouth shut, yet she chose the worst fucking time to tell Kaila the truth! I could've killed the bitch where she stood.

"Nigga, Kaila been done with your ass anyway. Do you

really think she was going to accept your proposal? You're a whole clown out here, and you treat her like those big-ass red shoes they walk around in."

"Shut the fuck up, Ann! You were the one who she called her sister, but look at how you did her. Yo' hoe ass gave it up too fucking easily. All it took for you to be disloyal to the one person who had your back through all y'all bullshit was some money and dick? You're fucking pathetic. Drop the kids off to my mama's house and kill your fucking self!"

"Yadda, yadda, ya—whatever you say, Charvo. Yo' ass was also disloyal, so let's jump in this sinking ship together. You knew exactly who I was and my situation when you approached me. Yo' ass is just as wrong as—" Feeling my phone vibrate in my pocket, I raised a hand to halt her words.

I quickly pulled my phone out, praying that Kaila was calling me back. I had tried to reach her over twenty times, but eventually, the calls started going directly to voicemail, so I gave up.

Green's name scrolled across the top of the screen, instantly making me feel sick. I thought about declining the call because I had a bad feeling, but I swiped the screen to answer it.

"Charvo... please come get me! I got a flat—" Alexia cried through the phone before I heard shuffling on the other end.

"Who the fuck is this playing on my phone?" I barked into the iPhone.

"Nigga, shut yo' bitch ass up! Send yo' location before we pop this bitch in the brain."

"My-my... what you mean? What the fuck is going on?" I stuttered.

"Scary ass nigga over here stuttering and shit. What's your location, nigga? I know you heard me the first time. This bitch over here has more heart than you. I see why you got her on your team."

"Don't you fuck niggas lay a hand on her. We can meet up, but I'm not sending my location."

"See, I thought you would try to have some kind of common sense in this situation, but from the way you moving and how you're speaking, I can tell we are going to have to play this shit our way. That was your baby mama and kids in that nice ass white Suburban leaving Disney World today, right? Lil thick shit with the bright red locs? They got on those matching family shirts, correct?"

"Nigga, what the fuck my family got to do with this?" I barked into the phone.

"Whoa, whoa, calm down. I thought you were the one calling plays." The nigga laughed in my ear. "You can either drop the location in the next... three minutes, or you'll get a text from this phone with the location of the bodies. Your choice."

"Wait, hold up—what more do you want from me? She had all the work in her car. If y'all got her, it ain't shit else needed from me."

"Nah, nigga, we need everything. That little travel bag she gave you, make sure you have that shit when we get there. Tick tock, motherfucker."

As soon as the call ended, I ran to the first trashcan I saw and emptied the contents of my stomach. Pepperann was behind me, rubbing my back to try to calm me down, but I was too distraught to push her away from me.

"What happened, Charvo? Who was that on the phone?" Once I finally stopped throwing up, she fired off question after question.

"Don't fucking worry about who that was on the phone. What you need to be doing is calling Kaila to find out where she is with the truck. She has some shit that belongs to me, and thanks to you, she's not answering the phone."

"If she's not answering for you, what the hell makes you think she'll answer for—" My hand went smooth across her face before she could finish her sentence. I hated when I had to show these bitches who they were fucking with.

"I don't want excuses, only solutions," I said before stomping away from her.

Watching the hours tick by had me antsy as I sat inside the motel room. Instead of dropping my location, I made Pepperann help me get the house packed up, and we got the fuck out of there. I sent her and the kids back to the hotel I had already taken care of for this trip while I lay low, trying to figure out my next move. The last of the ten bands I brought with me on this trip was dwindling quickly, and I didn't have a whip to get out of the city. Since I wasn't trying to leave a paper trail for anyone to find me, I refused to get a rental.

I was scrolling through my phone, looking at pictures of Kaila and the kids we'd taken over the years when I got an incoming FaceTime from her. Initially, I thought my mind was playing tricks on me, but when I answered and saw her chunky face appear on the screen, my heart slowed a bit.

"Charvo, where is our stuff? I'm at the house to get it, but it's nothing here."

"Kaila, baby...I had to clear out of there. The owners contacted me and told me there were some issues that they needed to take care of. I had to pack up everything and get a motel for the time being. Listen, that shit wasn't supposed to go down like that. You know I love you and the kids more than anything in the world. Look, I got the ring." Fumbling through my pockets, I pulled out the real engagement ring that I had for her. "You know how Ann is. She was just joking." I laughed, trying to ease the tension of the conversation.

When I looked back at the screen, I realized she had set the phone down because all I could see was the ceiling. A nigga had just poured his heart out, and she didn't even give me a moment to listen to what I had to say.

I watched as a hand went over the camera before picking up the phone. I was frozen at the sight of some linebacker-built nigga on the other end of the phone, staring back at me. The nigga smirked at me before turning the camera around and showing me my family walking out of the vacation home.

"Are you ready to tell us where you at?" His voice came through as the camera flipped back around to him.

"Nigga, who the fuck are you, and what are you doing with my bitch and my kids?? I know she ain't got another nigga around my kids already!!"

"That, she does, fuck nigga. Watch how you address her," he corrected me. "I'm about to take them to a real vacation spot. I bet your broke ass got this shit on Groupon." He chuckled.

"I play about a lot of shit, but my family ain't it! I swear to God, when I lay hands on you, it's a wrap for all you niggas."

"The same way you did your cousin?"

"I didn't—yeah, fuck nigga! The same way that slime ass nigga got handled. I'm on all that," I lied, trying to get one up on him.

The nigga flipped the camera around as he walked out of the house and to Kaila's truck. I watched as he opened the door for my motherfucking kids, then Kaila's hoe ass was standing there smiling in his face.

"Kaila! Who is this nigga, yo'? You fucking tweaking if you

think I'm going to let you have my kids around anyone but me. Give her the phone. I know she can hear me."

"She doesn't want to talk right now." He laughed. "My partners should be pulling up on you in a few. The way this new technology and shit works is crazy."

Realizing the nigga must have had some tracking shit on me because of my dumbass answering the call, my heart thumped loudly in my chest. I heard someone banging on the other side of the door as the FaceTime ended, and I knew I had been caught.

CHAPTER NINE
ASHONTE NEGRON

"Ashonte! Get up and open the door." My mom was banging on my bedroom door at the crack of dawn. I had just gotten in the house at four in the morning, and I could still taste the tequila on my tongue. I wasn't in the mood for her games.

"I'm sick, Ma, go away!" I yelled back before putting a pillow over my head to drown out the noise.

"Ashonte, if I have to kick this fucking door off the hinges, I will. Get your black ass up and open it now!!"

Kicking the blankets off, I forced myself out of bed and stomped to the door. When I snatched it open, my mom stood there with KJ on her hip. I was sure my confused expression spoke before words could leave my mouth.

"Here, I have to go to work, and you need to spend time with your son. Everything he needs is in the other room down the hall. Don't call me if he needs something. Call his dad." She passed KJ to me and didn't look back as she walked down the hallway and bent the corner to leave for work.

I'd been at my mom's house for almost a week, and most of

my days were spent sleeping until the sun went down, then getting up and going out to get drunk. Tyree was still ignoring my calls, and he hadn't posted anything on his social media accounts lately, so I had no idea what he was doing. I was tempted to go back to the house to see if he was there, but I didn't need the nigga turning up on my ass again.

KJ entered the world almost four years ago, and since the day I was discharged from the hospital, his father has had full custody of him. Keith knew I wasn't ready to be a parent when I found out I was pregnant, but I was also against having an abortion. I had watched too many videos of black women getting fucked up during the procedure, which led to them not being able to have children when they eventually became ready. Not wanting to risk messing up my reproductive system, I let Keith know that I would have the baby, but he would be the one to raise it.

Years ago, our families came together to throw us an extravagant baby shower to welcome the new addition, but I walked out in the middle of the celebration. I felt fake as fuck being there, knowing I had already gotten the paperwork to sign over my parental rights notarized and had the copies packed in my hospital bag for Keith when the time came.

KJ came into the world screaming loudly, and I remembered the sound of his voice piercing my ears. One of the nurses tried to place him on my chest for skin-to-skin contact, but I didn't want any of those bodily fluids to get on me. The moment they cleaned me up, I called Keith and told him his package was ready. I knew it was messed up for me to not call him when I went into labor, but I didn't need him in my space while I was going through it. Our relationship had come to an end after Keith made me choose between our family or being by myself. I would always and forever choose me; a nigga and a baby would never come before me.

"I'm hungry, Shonte," KJ whispered. He tried to lay his head on my shoulder, but I quickly set him down on his feet and told him to follow me to the kitchen.

I was thankful to see the plate wrapped on top of the stove that my mom had prepared before her departure. It was two pancakes with a few slices of bacon and breakfast potatoes. I threw the food in the microwave and told him to go to the fridge to make himself something to eat while I headed for the restroom. My head was still pounding, and my bladder was on fire from all the liquor I'd consumed just a few short hours prior.

While sitting on the toilet, I heard a loud scream come from the kitchen, startling me. I took my time wiping myself and then washing my hands before I walked back to the kitchen to see what had happened.

The cabinet with the cups was wide open, and a mug was shattered on the kitchen floor. KJ was on the ground screaming, and I saw a small piece of glass on one of his toes.

"What were you doing? How did you get the cabinet open? Stop all that crying. Little boys don't cry like that," I reprimanded him.

"My foot," he cried louder. "You told me to get my own juice." His breathing was heavy, and his whiny ass words were aggravating the fuck out of me since he was still crying.

"Don't move. Let me go get my house shoes," I told him and rushed off to get my slippers.

By the time I made it back, KJ was sitting up, still crying, and his chest was heaving up and down. He pointed to his foot so I could look at the small fragments of glass that had gotten into it, but I wasn't sure what to do. I picked him up from the floor and sat him on top of one of the counters to examine it closer. I knew my mother kept a first aid kit somewhere in the house, so I could get this out quickly, put a bandage on it, then sit him in front of the television so I could take a damn nap. I was too tired for this shit.

Using a pair of tweezers that I cleaned with rubbing alcohol, I took my time removing the glass from his foot and watched as the blood quickly oozed out of the tiny wound.

"You're going to be okay," I told him as I started applying pressure to stop the bleeding.

"It still hurts." He groaned in pain.

"You just cut it. Why would you expect it to stop hurting immediately?"

"Call my daddy or my nana. I want to go home." KJ wiped his eyes, trying to calm himself down.

"Stop all this crying. Big boys don't cry like this. You got hurt, you're bleeding, but you're okay, so suck it up." I applied pressure to his toe to stop the bleeding as he squeamishly tried to get away from me. "If you move again, I'm not putting a bandaid on it. You need to sit still so we can get this done," I warned sternly.

"I want my mommy," KJ cried softly. Staring at the little boy, I prayed he wasn't talking about me.

"Whoever that is needs to come and get you." I scoffed.

KJ didn't say another word as I cleaned up his toe and bandaged it before having him sit on a towel in front of the living room television to eat. Getting comfortable on the couch, I unlocked my phone to check my notifications and social media notifications.

I had a text message from an unsaved number. Since I had blocked Barbie's number and the other two bird brains, I figured it was one of them playing on my phone. The message included a screenshot from a social media story post. In the picture, Tyree was with a fat bitch on his lap, and I saw a pool in the background. He was flashing all thirty-two of his fucking teeth in the bitch's face like she was a damn dentist.

"What the fuck is this?" I sat up on the couch and quickly tapped Tyree's contact to FaceTime him. He had some nerve being out with another bitch when we still had unfinished business between us.

The phone only rang twice before I got a message that he was unavailable. I could feel my anger ready to spill over as I typed out a page-long text, cursing him out and explaining how fucked up it was for him to throw me out without letting me fully explain my actions. The fact that he already had another bitch in his face let me know that she must've been in the picture for a long time.

Just when a nigga thought he was beating me at his own game, I had all the mother fucking cheat codes. The sweetest revenge for me was getting one up on a nigga, and my one up was to always get to the motherfucking bag.

"Put on your shoes so we can go somewhere real quick."

"Are you taking me home?" he asked with bright eyes.

"If you remember where you live, that'll be our first stop!"

Using my mom's old car, we were blazing down the highway to Tyree's house in Brickell. Since his ass was on a damn vacation, I was sure my key still worked at his house, so I was going to get what was rightfully mine. I knew his cameras were active twenty-four-seven, and according to him, they were among the best on the market, but today, I was fully prepared to call his bluff.

"Stay in the car. I'll be right back," I told KJ as I put the windows up, turned the car off, and locked the doors behind me. He was crying about something again, but I quickly walked away, ignoring him.

Before using my key, I knocked on the door a few times to see if anyone was home. Tyree had started parking in the garage again, but I couldn't access it without the clicker that remained inside the car he got me a few years ago, which I was sure he had locked in the garage. The doorbell camera didn't light up either, so I knew he had most likely not charged it because that was something I used to do for him.

Sliding the key into the lock, I prayed it would still work. A devilish smirk graced my face as I heard the lock slide back. I was inside Tyree's and my home and headed straight for the guest bedroom. I knew he kept a safe in that room because I'd witnessed him go in there a few times with bundles of money and then walk out empty-handed. I might've acted green to whatever he had going on because I wanted him to trust that I wasn't with him for the money, but I knew what type of time he was on.

After pulling out drawers, removing pictures from the walls, and sliding furniture out of my way, I found myself empty-handed. With every step I took in that bedroom, I racked my brain, trying to figure out where the fuck he kept the money.

"Take another fucking step, and I'm blowing that plastic ass wig off your head." My hands shot up as I heard the gun being cocked, and I slowly turned around.

Starja was staring at me with menacing eyes, and her gun was trained on me.

"I was—I came to get the rest of my stuff. I don't want no problems, Starja. You don't even have to tell Tyree I came by," I pleaded, arms still raised.

"You don't tell me what the fuck to do. I'm only going to ask you this once, and if I don't like your answer, I hope your mama is ready to fry some damn fish for your funeral arrangements. What are you doing in my house?"

Her question got an eyebrow raise out of me. "This is me and Tyree's house. I've been living here with him for the last few years. I know he tells you every fucking detail of his life, so the fact that you're acting like this is your shit is not a good look." Although I had a gun fixed on me, that did nothing to hide the fear coursing through my body.

"Hmm... that's why all those SwapShop ass clothes were in that dusty closet. It makes sense now." She chuckled. "Well, y'all don't live here anymore. My baby daddy gave me the keys and got all y'all shit out of here, so this isn't the place for you to be. I suggest you get a move on before I have to shoot your ass for trespassing."

"My key still works. You sound stupid as fuck. This right here is my shit! Tyree bought this house for me. See, the problem is, you and that other fat ass baby mama of his think y'all run *my* man. I'm the one and only queen of this castle. What I suggest you do is put that fucking gun down and run a fair one with me. You ain't shit without that gun; I promise you that. Y'all turn y'all noses up at me every chance y'all get, but fuck all that."

She stepped toward me, and my heart rate rapidly increased as I saw her finger inch closer to the trigger.

"I never did like you, so I'm not even going to sit here and play nice with you. The only thing you can say about Vanessa and me is that we're fat, but guess what bitch? Our baby daddy loves it. He's still paying all our bills, taking care of our kids, funding our businesses and our lifestyles. You don't even deserve a man like Tyree, not even when he was at his worst. You will never fit into our picture-perfect puzzle. And from that video floating around on Twitter with you and them nasty ass bitches shoving plastic in your dirty ass hole and then in your mouth, you're the last bitch to talk out the side of your neck about anything of his belonging to you."

Paying close attention to her grip on the gun as she spoke, I reached for it but underestimated her strength and speed. She hauled back and smacked the shit out of me, causing me to see stars.

"You want your one? Let's go, bitch!" She yanked me by my hair with one hand, then her other hand wound around until it landed square in my face.

"Let me get up," I commanded while struggling to hold my own.

Starja stepped back, giving me space to stand up. She switched the gun's safety before placing it beside her on the bed. My eyes quickly scanned the distance between me and her compared to my distance away from the door. This big bitch was going to give me a run for my money if we went head-up, and I didn't have a weapon, so the next best thing came to mind. I darted for the door, and the moment I crossed the threshold, someone stuck their arm out in front of me, causing me to fly backward and lose my balance.

"I swear to God I hate this bitch, Starja." Vanessa wore a disgusted expression as she stared down at me. Starja joined her as she mentioned that the police were on the way.

"Her stupid ass ain't even worth putting a bullet in." Starja scoffed as she walked outside.

The police sirens were growing louder, and I knew I had no choice but to face the music. Vanessa remained planted in the hallway until I got up to make my way to the exit.

Walking outside, I was shocked to see the paramedics rushing away from my car with a small figure on the stretcher. I frantically ran over to my car. It was only then that I remembered KJ was in it. The temperature outside was close to one hundred degrees. I had fucked up, not even thinking about how hot it could've gotten in the car while he waited on me.

"Ma'am, is this your vehicle? What were you doing in that house?"

"My son! What the fuck happened to my son?" Tears filled my eyes as I dropped to my knees. I could no longer make out what the police were saying to me as one of them got me to the ground and placed me in handcuffs.

As I was aided to an upright position, Tyree approached.

"That's your kid, Ashonte?" I couldn't hear his words, but I read his lips.

Dropping my gaze to the ground, I told the police officers to hurry up and get me out of there.

CHAPTER TEN

KAILA MOFFETT

"All of a sudden, you think you're too good to come to work these days? You already took last week off, and now look at you. On the day you're supposed to return to the office, you're not even here on time. You are such a disgrace, Kaila Moffett, and I hope they fire your ugly, black, fat neck, ham hock built ass the moment you walk through the door!" Caroline's voice echoed through the small office as I played the voice message for my direct supervisor. This wasn't the first time I'd reported Caroline's harassment and sinister ways, but this was the first time that I had solid proof of the fuckery she had been keeping up.

Over the last few months, her behavior had gotten more unhinged, and now it seemed that she had lost all her fucking marbles, leaving me that damn voice message. I was pulling into the parking lot when she repeatedly called my phone. I didn't answer because I knew I'd be walking in shortly. Maybe she thought she ended the call before leaving the message, but after listening to it, everyone in the room knew it was intentional.

"I know that you all have to go through your procedures and protocols, but I'm letting you know now that I refuse to continue working with her under these conditions. There are underlying issues for which only she has the answers. I love my job, but my peace and sanity come before all else." I grabbed my phone off Andrew's desk.

"We are going to get this resolved, Kaila. I sincerely apologize that you have been dealing with this, and I wish we could've handled this sooner."

"Me too, but I appreciate you wanting a resolution. Do you need anything else from me? I did email you a copy, and I included HR in the email."

"Okay. I am approving you to work from home for the remainder of the week. We will keep you in the loop as to the outcome of this unfortunate situation. Again, my sincerest apologies for not handling this before it reached this point. Let me walk you to your car."

"That's okay. I need a few things from my desk, so I'll be able to work at home. I'm sure I'll be okay." I half-smiled before excusing myself.

Caroline's face was the first one I saw when the elevator doors opened on the first floor. She was standing there as if she was waiting specifically for me.

"Did you go and run your fat ass lips to those white people upstairs?" Her raspy whisper was like nails against a chalkboard in my ears.

"I will never understand your reason for fucking with me outside of you being old, grumpy, and miserable, but you got it, Caroline. I wish you all the best," I spoke as I made my way to my cubicle, not bothering to turn back to see if she was following me.

"Miserable? Little girl, I've been on this earth twice as long as you've been alive. The only thing miserable about my life is having to work with your fat ass! You can't even walk up the fucking stairs, but you're calling me old and miserable. Kiss the deepest parts of my black ass, you nasty bitch! Next time, I hope that neighbor of yours shoots the brains out of your fucking kids!" She seethed.

All my self-control lost its way as I turned around to show this old lady who she was fucking with. Initially, I was joking when I said she must be losing her marbles, but after hearing her speak ill on my kids, I knew I was speaking facts.

"Hold on, Kaila. I was standing right here the entire time. Caroline, go upstairs to HR right now! Kaila, please get what you need and head out."

"You don't fucking tell me what to do! You are not the boss of me either. I'm not going nowhere," she raged. "I've been at this company longer than anyone else in this fucking building! I should be the fucking CEO. I should be the one running this fucking show."

Andrew was on his phone calling for backup while I maneuvered through my desk to gather files and other necessary items for me to work from home. As I got the last of what I needed, I heard people hurrying to get to the scene. Caroline hadn't stopped cursing and ranting about how terrible the organization had become. Watching her go from being one of the highest-paid employees there due to her tenure to losing her job over a meltdown was insane.

I shook my head as I walked through the crowd to leave the building. She continued to shout obscenities at my back, but I didn't give her any more of my attention. If I caught her old ass on the street, though, that would be another story, especially after what she said about my kids.

Our nonprofit was in with the police department, so I wasn't surprised to see a few of their patrol cars pulling into the parking lot with their sirens off. One of the white people probably called them after seeing that old, mad black woman losing her shit. I didn't bother speaking to them. Before they could exit their cars, I was leaving the parking lot and heading to run a few errands since it wasn't time for me to get the kids yet.

There was an apartment complex in Pembroke Pines that I had been researching for the last few weeks. Online, it said they didn't have any vacancies, but I figured I'd still stop in and try my luck.

An Asian woman greeted me but threw me off a bit because she also looked black. I tried not to stare, but her beautiful features and deep purple hair had my undivided attention.

"Good morning. How may I help you?" She smiled. Looking down at my watch, I saw that it was only a little after 9:00 A.M.

"Yes, good morning. I'm sorry to just come in like this. I was wondering if you all had any vacancies. I'm looking to move with my children, and the one-bedroom is in my price range."

I knew a one-bedroom apartment wasn't big enough for me and the kids, but until I could get us into a better situation, this would have to do. I planned to buy three twin-sized beds for the bedroom, and I'd sleep in the living room. We didn't have company often; now that Pepperann and I wouldn't be speaking again, I was pretty sure I'd never have company again.

"Give me a moment. Let me check the system," she said before looking at the computer screen in front of her.

I had already prepared myself for a long speech about them not having anything available and her apologizing, so I picked up my keys off the counter and shouldered my purse as I prepared to leave.

"Alright... well, I have good news and bad news." She paused.

"I always like the bad news first." I shrugged.

"At this time, we don't have any one-bedroom apartments available, but we do have a two-bedroom apartment with a flex room. I know you mentioned a one-bedroom being in your budget, so I'm not sure if this one will work for you. But I can take you to see it if you wish."

Mentally calculating my budget, I did have enough to stretch for a couple hundred more, but that was the most I could do.

"Honestly, I can only spare about two hundred dollars over what I had calculated for the one bedroom. I don't want to waste your time."

"I think you should walk with me and check it out." She winked and smiled before pointing to a closed door behind me. I quickly picked up the hint she was throwing and proceeded outside to wait for her to show me the unit.

"My name is Spring, by the way. What's yours?"

"I'm Kaila. Thank you for taking time out to do this." We shook hands.

"I couldn't say too much in there, but we are getting ready to run a rent special at the start of next month. The first three months of rent will be half off, and if you sign a twenty-four-month lease, we partner with a community organization that has a rental program that sets you up for homeownership. I understand it may be a bit of a stretch for you to pay the full amount of rent once that does kick in, but our community partner is there to help," Spring explained.

Although it sounded good, it also sounded too damn good. I was looking around for the camera crew to jump out and tell me that I was being pranked.

"And how much does this mysterious community partner charge?"

"It's a nonprofit, and they don't charge a thing. I can connect you with our point of contact so they can discuss more details with you."

"I'd appreciate that." I nodded.

Spring unlocked the door to the unit, and as we entered, I pictured my kids' shoes on a rack near the door as they rumbled through the apartment that would become our home. The fresh paint and carpeted floors made the place beautiful. It looked as if it had never been lived in.

"So, this is the flex space I was telling you about. Many of our tenants use this space as an office; a few have converted it to a third bedroom. How many children do you have, if you don't mind me asking?"

"I have three," I said.

"And you wanted a one-bedroom? If you think I was going to let you apply for a one-bedroom with three children, you're crazy!" she said, and we both laughed. "I'm also willing to run a few numbers and talk to our manager to see what we can do. I don't know your situation, but I can feel your energy, and I want to help out in any way I can."

"What would I need to do to get started?" At times, I was a skeptic, but I stayed prayed up, and I knew when God placed me in the right positions at the right times. So, I wouldn't let this blessing pass me by.

After touring the unit, I was more than sure that I would be signing a lease soon. I was already planning a few ways I could make extra income to cover the additional costs I'd have to take on, but I knew I could make it work. I met the property owner, and Spring introduced him as her father-in-law. I was happy to see a black man thriving within our community. They could've gotten the apartment complex

built in a more affluent area to serve a different type of popu-
lation, but they chose to have it in an area that caters to our
people. After speaking with the property manager, Vonzel, I
learned they had several other properties throughout Dade
and Broward counties. Their community involvement introduced better opportunities to those who were ready to
elevate their lives.

Spring asked me to come by the office on Wednesday to
return the application, and she managed to waive the fee for
me. I left with a new outlook on my children and my future. It
was going to take some time for us to get this right, but for
them, I would do whatever it took.

I decided to head to the house to have a little more alone
time before picking up the kids from school. I knew I should've
been home and logged into the system to at least pretend I was
working, but after the bullshit with Caroline, Andrew would
have to understand that I needed some me time.

Charvo still hadn't returned to our home since the kids and
I returned from Orlando. I had been hesitant about returning
home and facing him, but I had a new sense of purpose
regarding my peace and happiness. I knew and accepted that
he was no longer the person for me. No matter how badly I
wanted to spend the rest of my days with him, he didn't want
the same with me, and I was okay with that.

To kill time before I needed to pick up the kids, I started
dinner and researched the cost of a moving company. Since I
had purchased the majority of the furniture in our house, it
was all coming with me. Charvo wanted to be out here on
some stupid shit, so I would leave his stupid ass alone to figure
his life out.

"Who was that nigga you had around my kids, Kaila?" As I
sat at the dining room table with my MacBook in front of me,
Charvo came into the house limping. One of his arms was in a

sling, his left eye had a patch over it, and there was a huge knot in the center of his forehead.

"What the hell happened to you?" I exclaimed while taking in his appearance.

"Don't ask me no fucking questions! I was all over Orlando looking for you and the kids. You really left me up there, Kaila? So that's what type of time you on now?" he raged.

"Before I get upset and black your other eye, I suggest you lower your motherfucking tone and watch how you talk to me," I warned.

"My shit not black. I got in a fucking car accident and got a few bumps and bruises. But don't sit here and act like you didn't hear my question. Who was that nigga? We've been through too much shit for it to go down the way it did. You know I would never do anything like that to humiliate you, Kaila. I love you, and I mean that from the bottom of my heart. I want us to make this work for the kids—"

"And that's our problem. We sit in this bullshit of a relationship because of the kids. We've been unhappy for a long time, yet we continue to put up a facade like everything is good. It's not, Charvo, and it hasn't been for a long time. I can't even remember the last time we hugged or kissed. We haven't had sex in over three years. I was hoping you would get tired of me holding out on you and leave, but that's my fault for even giving you the benefit of the doubt."

"We can start this shit over, Kaila. Do everything the right way," he pleaded.

"I don't want to, Charvo. I'm done. I chose me this time. I'm tired of being unhappy. My kids deserve a happy mother, and that's what I will give them."

"If you think you're leaving me to be with that other nigga, you got me fucked up! And you're dead ass wrong for having him around my kids when I don't even know the nigga. How long have you been fucking him? You are not getting it from me, so who's been taking my place?"

"How long have you been fucking her? That bitch made it crystal clear what y'all had going on. And you need to be fucking for real right now. The nigga had me and the kids held hostage because of that fucking bag you thought you stashed in my truck. I might've acted blind to the bullshit while we enjoyed the remainder of our time in Orlando, but I knew exactly what was going on. The kids and I had the time of our lives, and guess what—it was all on his dime. You can sit up there and create whatever fucking scenario you want in your head, but I didn't know him before Friday."

"Nah, that doesn't even sound right. Just tell me how long you've been fucking him. I promise I won't get mad," Charvo argued.

"I'm done having this conversation with you. I'm sure you know exactly how to find him if you want to ask him that question. I'm going to get the kids. One of us has to be the responsible adult." Rolling my eyes, I snatched my keys and purse off the table near the front door before making my exit.

By the time Wednesday rolled around, my anxiety was through the roof. Charvo and I had managed to cut all communication, which seemed to be the best thing for us. I knew he was low-key trying to get a rise out of me by talking loudly on the phone to whatever bitch was blowing up his phone at all hours of the night, but it was no longer my business. Today was the day Spring told me to head back to the apartments so I could turn in the application and find out my next steps.

As soon as I dropped the kids off for school, I headed back home, took care of a few things for work, and then went up to the rental office while on my usual midday break. Working from home was turning out to be much better than I'd imagined. As long as I was getting my tasks completed and keeping Andrew updated on my progress, he didn't have a problem with me working remotely.

"Good afternoon, Spring! It's nice to see you again," I greeted her after she welcomed me in with the brightest smile on her face.

"I'm so glad you came back today. Sometimes, I tell people to return on a certain day, then I don't hear from them for months. I've got some great news for you. I think you should sit down for this," she gushed, and I quickly slid into one of the open seats in front of her desk. "So, Vonzel made a few phone calls to our community partners to see what we can do to make living here more manageable for you, and we found a partner who is willing to pay half of your rent for the duration of the twenty-four-month lease."

"Are you serious right now, Spring? Please don't play with me like that." Tears rushed to my eyes as I struggled to keep my emotions under wraps.

"I don't know you like that, so believe me when I say that's not something I would play about. Our community partner is supposed to arrive in the next hour or so if you have time and want to meet with them. There are a few specific terms and conditions, but they coincide with a few of the things we already have in place. I'll give you a moment to get yourself together." She passed me the box of tissues on her desk, and the silent tears of joy no longer had a reason to remain captive.

The last few months had been filled with prayer sessions and time for God and me to figure out what I would do with my life. I was tired of feeling defeated and unloved. I was tired of being surrounded by people who didn't have the best intentions for me. Although I now felt alone more than at any other time in my life, I felt as if God had put me in this position so I could see that I could overcome the obstacles stacked against me on my own.

"Thank you so much, Spring. I'm honestly speechless." I sniffled.

"I told you I felt your energy, and I sincerely wanted to help however I could. This will be an incredible new start for you and your children."

Spring reviewed the forms I brought in, and then we went over the twenty-four-month lease page by page so she could ensure I understood the particular terms and conditions of living there. Two years sounded like a long time, but I felt that was more than enough time for me to get into grind mode so that when the time was up, I'd be ready for homeownership.

"Here comes our community partner. I want to make the introduction." Spring winked.

I stood and smoothed out the wrinkles in the outfit I wore. Since I was working from home, I kept it casual with a pair of flowy pants and the matching body suit, which snapped at the crotch. I was usually confident about my appearance whenever I stepped out, but for some reason, the butterflies swarming in my stomach were increasing by the second. Spring entered her boss's office first, and I followed right behind.

"Mr. Roman, I'd like you to meet the tenant we told you about on Monday. This is Kaila Moffett. Kaila, this is Tyree Roman, the owner of Roman's Legacy.

The smile on my face dropped at the sight of him and was quickly replaced with embarrassment.

CHAPTER ELEVEN
TYREE ROMAN

"I'm not sure what this goofy ass bitch of yours has going on, but if she doesn't get her ass out of my fucking house, I'm going to blow her brains out, Tyree!" Starja screamed into the phone, causing me to pull it away from my ear and place her on speaker.

"Calm down and tell me what's going on, Starja. I don't have a bitch, so I don't know who you're talking about."

"The skinny ass crackhead. Why is she in my house? I just watched this hoe on my doorbell camera. I thought you had the locks changed before I moved in. How did her key still work on my front door, Tyree?"

"Damn... I've been meaning to get that taken care of. I'm sorry. It's been a lot going on. I'll handle it. Are you home now?"

"No, me and Vanessa are doing some last-minute shopping since we had to take an unplanned trip at your request. We are on the way to the house right now, though. She's been in there for almost twenty minutes already. We got the cameras open. She seems to be focused on the downstairs guest room. That's the only room she went into once she got inside."

"Aight. If you beat me there, please keep your cool, Starja. I'll talk to her."

"Yo' ass better beat me there," she remarked before banging on me.

Keem and I were discussing the outcome of the Orlando trip. He was doing most of the talking while I sat back and listened. Truthfully, I didn't like how the nigga moved. Instead of letting the nigga Charvo meet his maker, he let the nigga free after I beat his ass, but only under the condition of him not crossing our paths anymore. I knew that was going to be a waste of time because I needed Kaila in my life, even if I had to run through that fuck nigga to make it happen.

"You know that nigga Green still fighting for his life? Even though Doc made it clear that he would never breathe on his own again, that young bull still holding on."

"I'm sure that nigga wants some get back. Your own blood tried to wipe you off the map? Nigga, keep me alive so I can get my revenge. Then I'll be ready to go. Don't be surprised if that's exactly what he does. You don't want to get caught up in the crossfire if that does happen."

"I'm good, nigga. You can bet that. Alexia did her part; we got all the work back and then some. I ain't worried about shit else."

"I hear you, but I need you to take some time to get all of this under control. I'm not coming out of retirement anytime soon. The only reason I stepped back this time was because this was the first time you've had to lean on me. Let this be a lesson—get your team together, stop letting these young snake niggas in the circle, and keep all the fuck shit to a minimum. I did it for years and never had to deal with bullshit like this. It's no excuse for you," I lectured.

I knew he didn't want to hear what I had to say, but I needed him to understand that I had given up this lifestyle for a reason. I put in my time and held shit down. He needed to put on his big-boy shoes and make shit happen.

"*I hear you. I've got everything under control now. I appreciate you for looking out. It's a small thing to a giant.*" The black bag Keem placed on the table made a loud thud when he set it down.

"*Appreciate you, but I gotta jet. Sounds like Ashonte got herself into some bullshit at Starja's house.*"

"*Damn, nigga, it's always drama with them,*" Keem commented as he stood.

"*Nah, you only know about the drama because that's the only thing I tell you about. Outside of all that, life is good. I honestly can't complain. We'll get up, though.*"

After we dapped each other up, I left Keem's house and sped through the neighborhood to get to the highway. I already knew that Starja and Vanessa would make it to her house before me, but I prayed she didn't take that girl's life. Although I wanted her out of mine, she didn't need to catch a bullet over what could possibly be a misunderstanding. When I decided that I was completely done with Ashonte, instead of renting the house out to a stranger, I offered it to one of my baby's mothers to help them out. Vanessa told me things were getting serious with her new man, and she wanted to hold off on moving, so Starja decided to take it.

Traffic on 95 had me driving twenty miles an hour as I switched in and out of lanes, trying to make it to my exit. By the time I got off the highway, a line of police cars was zooming past me, headed in the same direction as Starja's house. I was right behind them as they headed to the community. Before we made it to the house, I saw an ambulance backed into the driveway along with a fire truck and at least seven other police cruisers.

I parked down the street and jogged up to the house. At the same time, a small child was being wheeled away on a stretcher. Ashonte was screaming for someone to save her son, and I struggled to process her words.

"*That's your kid, Ashonte?*" I barked, but she was too distraught to answer my question. "*Is that her kid?*" I stopped one of the paramedics who had just walked away from Ashonte's mom's car, which was parked in the driveway near the front door.

"Yes, sir, she left the baby in the car. He was unresponsive when we arrived, but we managed to get him breathing again. Will you be coming with us to the hospital?" I could only stare at the woman as she awaited my response.

"Nah..." was the only answer I could give.

Pacing back and forth in the driveway, anger loomed in my eyes as I watched Ashonte get placed into the back of a police cruiser and hauled off. That kid was at least three or four years old, and she had never mentioned having a child for the entirety of our relationship.

"Tyree."

I looked toward the porch when Vanessa called my name and motioned for me to enter the house.

When I got inside, I was thankful that the house was still intact. I figured Ashonte came over to trash the place or pop up on me to wreak havoc.

"She only came in this room. Do you know what she may have been looking for?" Vanessa whispered as we stood outside the guest bedroom while police officers collected evidence and took pictures of the scene.

On more than one occasion, Ashonte had seen me walk into that room to put things away in my 'stash.' Little did she know, a hidden passageway led to a panic room where I had been putting everything. The bitch may have been smarter than I thought.

"I have a feeling, but we'll talk."

We headed for the living room to check on Starja, who had been talking to police officers and giving them the camera footage from the security system. I expected her to be distraught and put on a show for the police officers, but the rapid bouncing in her leg let me know that she was pissed.

When the police left an hour later, Starja cursed me out for not changing the locks sooner. The kit I ordered was in the garage, so I *started working on that while she talked my ear off about not handling Ashonte sooner. I thought she would heed my warning when I kicked her out of the house, but again, I had to admit to my baby mamas that I was wrong.*

Before leaving Starja's place, I did one more walkthrough to make sure Ashonte hadn't touched anything else in the house. Although the camera showed her going into one room, I needed to make sure.

I was walking out the door when they mentioned Kaila's name and asked when they'd be seeing her again. Shrugging my shoulders, I walked out to make it to another pressing matter.

I'd been searching the city high and low for Miss Kaila Moffett since she left the hotel with her children on Sunday afternoon. Before that moment, I knew exactly what I would say to her if I ever saw her again, but now that she stood before me, words seemed to evade me.

"It's nice to meet you officially, Miss Moffett. Come in and have a seat." I patted the empty seat beside me; my glare made her uncomfortable because she was doing everything she could to avoid my eyes.

"I can't stay long. I'm on my lunch break right now."

"How has work been since—" I stopped myself, not wanting to reveal too much of what we discussed during our weekend together.

"Work is work." She shrugged. "I'd like a little more information on the terms of the program. I agree with everything I saw on the lease. However, I want to ensure I understand what will be required of me. Spring did an amazing job of explaining everything to me, but I like to cover all the bases." She winked at me.

"Oh, see, your terms need to be updated a bit. That's what Vonzel and I discussed before you came in. Typically, this program is designed for people who haven't started their careers yet, or they may be at a point in life where they are figuring out what they actually want to do with their lives. Since you have those things figured out, we feel it may be best for you to continue with the twenty-four-month lease, but during that time, you have to sign up for school. Looking over your application, we noticed you listed a few colleges, but I didn't see a completion date. Did you, Vonzel?"

"I didn't." He shook his head.

"I don't see myself having time for schoolwork and my kids as a single parent. I've wanted to go back for a while now, but I don't have a support system that could help me through that process."

"So, what do you need? A babysitter or nanny a few times a week? An after-school program for the kids to join so you can have the time you need? Let me know. I want to make this doable for you."

"Are you serious right now?" She was smiling, but confusion lingered in her eyes.

"Let's connect her with Smoke's after-school program. I think that'll be good for her boys. Her daughter can work with Xoey at New Leaf. How many days a week would classes be?"

Vonzel sat back, scribbling in a notebook as he chuckled at me calling the shots while Kaila stared.

"Just give me clarity on one thing," she implored. "What bills of mine do you plan to pay to make all of this happen? With childcare comes additional costs. Afterschool activities require more driving, which requires more gas money for me to pick the kids up. Going to school requires longer nights, which may mean less time for cooking, cleaning, and homework with the kids. Do you see where I'm going?"

"The purpose of us discussing this right now is to determine what we can do to help make this easier for you. So far, I'm hearing you need a nanny for weeknights, your tank filled every Sunday to start your week off, and any bills you fall short on can be sent directly to me. Did I miss anything?"

"You didn't." She tittered as she stood. "Thank you all for your time. I don't know what type of operation y'all are running here, but I don't want any parts of it. You gentlemen have a nice day." Kaila walked out of the office without giving us another opportunity to speak.

"Spring will handle it," Vonzel assured me.

I was ready to get up and run after her to talk some sense into her. Maybe this shit did sound too sweet, but I knew she needed the help. I didn't want her baby daddy doing anything else for her since he was already fucking her over.

"Where do you know her from?" he asked.

"You know that nigga Keem had me tapped in last week, and shawty happened to get caught in the crossfire. I don't know her entire situation, but I do know that she needs to get away from the nigga she's with. He left her and her kids for dead on some scary shit. It was a fucked up situation, but we made the most of it. Starja and Vanessa brought my jits up there, and we made a weekend of it. Did the whole SeaWorld and Universal Studios theme parks. You know how I live my life, Vonzel, so it was out of place for me to connect with her and her kids so easily. She fits perfectly, though. That's the scary part."

"It sounds like your ass is ready to do more than help her out. From what I see, she's definitely your type. I hope she gets you away from that crackhead you've been dealing with." His mentioning Ashonte caused me to shake my head.

Everyone who knew me questioned what the hell I was doing with a bitch like her. From the moment we started kicking it, she'd tried to turn my life upside down, causing chaos between the kids' moms and me, complaining about working and me not breaking enough bread. Hindsight was 20/20 whenever I thought about our situation. I could admit that I had to take it to the chest when I walked in on her fucking a bitch in my home, but I needed to see that for me to be done.

"If she agrees to proceed with the lease, I'll pay her rent monthly. Just let me know if Spring can work her magic."

"I got you, bruh. Don't have her ass stressing you out and shit. You know how these women can be." We laughed as we slapped hands, and I went on my way.

The white Suburban was backed into the first parking spot, and the engine was running. As tempted as I was to walk over and speak to her one last time, I kept moving to my car.

"How are you doing this afternoon? I'm here to clean out the suite I was renting since the lease won't be renewed. I don't remember who I spoke to on the phone, but I called last week and was told I could get it cleaned out today." I spoke to the receptionist who sat behind a desk at the salon suites.

"Mr. Roman, yes, sir, we've been expecting you. We actually tried to call you earlier today. Ashonte Negron is here. She said you authorized her to keep the space for a few more months, so there is some confusion."

"I'm sorry, I didn't approve that. I'll go speak to her, and we'll be out of your way shortly." Tapping the desk lightly, I took brisk steps that had me barging into the suite in no time.

She had a client in the chair with her hair halfway done while another girl sat in a chair against the wall with a bonnet on her head as if she was waiting to be serviced.

"What the fuck you got going on, Ashonte? Get your shit and get these bitches the fuck up out of here. Yo' ass ain't been here in months now, and now you trying to work. A fucking joke, bruh."

"In front of my clients, Tyree? Are you serious right now?"

I was already snatching paintings and shit off the walls and tossing them into a pile beside the door.

"You keeping all this shit over here?" I popped open a large black trash bag and waited for her to answer my question.

"I'm not going anywhere, Tyree. Can you calm the fuck down and stop throwing my shit everywhere, please? I have clients right now. This is not how I run my business, and you know that."

"Now you want to talk about running a fucking business, Ashonte? Well, let's talk!" My voice boomed.

I was sure the property managers would be over to check us about the noise, but I didn't give a fuck. Since she wanted to play crazy, I was going to show her ass stupid.

"You had a child this entire time?"

Ashonte stared at me, trying to communicate with her eyes, but I was no longer on her time.

"I need y'all to go. I'll call you with a time I can finish your hair later today, and Tisha, come to my mom's house in the morning so I can do yours. I'm sorry for the inconvenience."

Both girls looked at her in disgust before they gathered their belongings and left the suite together. I could hear the one with her hair half-done talking shit under her breath.

As Ashonte stood in silence, I resumed throwing everything into the trash bag to get this over with. Ashonte had started crying and sniffling as I maneuvered around her, ignoring her crocodile tears.

"Tyree, please wait... hear me out," she pleaded.

"Answer my question, Ashonte. Was that your son who had to be rushed to the hospital?"

"I didn't want a child, Tyree. I didn't want to be pregnant. I had the baby, and his dad has had him since."

"You know how fucked up of a person you have to be to walk away from the child you birthed? How the fuck can you even live with yourself, not knowing how your child is doing? Then, when you had him in your care, you purposely left him in a hot car, and he almost fucking died! I wasn't out here tied down to nobody, Ashonte, no fucking body. Yet you came in regulating shit and trying to switch up my motion. Despite all of that, I was still ready to lock this shit down with you. Now, I realize that our entire situation was a fucking lie, Ashonte."

"It wasn't a lie. My feelings for you are genuine! I appreciate everything you do for me, Tyree. I was fucked up, and my mind wasn't clear because I had the wrong people in my ear about you. I've never been loved the way you love me, baby. I promise I can and will do better. I am going to get my shit together for you and my son. I want us to be a family. I'll do what I must to get along with your children and their moms. I've been extremely stressed and depressed, Tyree, and I've been taking it out on you. I sincerely apologize, and I promise I'll do better."

"Family? I don't want shit else to do with you, shawty. I gave yo' ass chance after chance to get your shit together and realize that I was different from anything you were used to, but you took advantage. And now you got a video of you getting a fucking train ran on you by two bitches all over the fucking internet, and you think that's the type of woman I want by my side? I suggest you get whatever you need out of here before I start making dumpster trips. This suite has been unused for months, so this sudden change of heart and desire to do right is a day late and a dollar short. I wish you all the best with your future endeavors, Ashonte, but our chapter is done."

"Tyree... please. Don't do this, baby," she begged as she tried to reach for me, but I stepped back. I didn't even want her touching me anymore.

"What else do you need, Ashonte?"

"I need you!"

"What else do you need from here? Ain't shit left to say about us. I need you to process that and understand it. I'm done talking about it. The only thing we need to do is get this suite cleaned out. I don't even care about trying to get the deposit back at this point. Grab what you need and get on, Ashonte."

"You act like you're so fucking innocent in all of this! I saw the pictures of you and that fat bitch by the fucking pool. You were smiling in her face and shit like you've been fucking her. Then you moved your ugly-ass baby mama into my house! You wanted me to be a pawn in your game, and all was well until you let them get into your head about me."

"Whatever you say, Ashonte. Less yapping, more packing."

I was all types of fuck niggas and pussy ass motherfuckers as she snatched up the essential things she needed and tossed them into her own garbage bags. Every few minutes, she would comment or ask a direct question, but I continued to ignore her as I pulled the last few things out of the suite and into the hallway to take to the dumpster.

After doing a final walk-through with one of the property managers, we agreed on the cost for all the damages and things they would have to replace before a new tenant moved in, and I paid off the difference. Instead of getting rid of the equipment, the property manager asked me to move everything into a storage room so they could have the equipment on hand for possible future tenants.

Taking the time to get this one last connection with Ashonte severed was more than I needed. The decision to have my name as the only one on the lease for the suite was a business move I was happy I made. We had no other legally binding obligations that would've made getting her out of my life more complex.

Starja's text message lit up my phone as I placed it into a cupholder inside my truck.

Starja: I'll take a Birkin or a Chanel bag, your choice. Love you, baby daddy.

Her message included a link to a *Baby Mama Number Three Background* file. Starja was a damn fool, but I also knew she wasn't blind. When I met Ashonte, I asked her to conduct a background check. Starja came back to me with pages of red flags and clear signs for me to leave her the fuck alone, but I ignored all of them. This time, I would take heed to the info she provided on Miss Kaila Moffett.

It was something about Kaila that I felt I needed in my life. Her vulnerability and brokenness were hard for me to process. I didn't think of myself as the kind of nigga who was out here saving women, but I was ready to pick up my cape from the dry cleaners for this one. Although her spirit was broken inside out, she remained strong. I wanted to be the one to show her that there was so much more to life than hurt and heartbreak.

During our unexpected time together in Orlando, Vanessa and Starja brought the kids up so I could take them out before they went on their week-long cruise vacation. Kaila fell right in step with Starja and Vanessa regarding keeping up with all the kids. There were times I looked at them, and they were all smiling and laughing as if they'd known each other for a lifetime. Despite what Kaila was going through, my children's mothers couldn't tell she was dealing with personal issues. Our children got along perfectly because they were all around the same age. Before our departure, Vanessa and Starja pulled me aside to pick my brain about her. I didn't want to tell them how I met her or that I had only met her a day before they arrived, but I was a man about mine and kept it real. Surprisingly, they both pressed me to get right with her. They also loved how she handled the kids and felt she would be an unproblematic addition to our family dynamic. Little did they know, my wheels were already turning.

The first thing I needed to do was solidify her being done with her fuck ass baby daddy. In Orlando, I wanted that nigga's head on a fucking platter by the time I finished beating his ass, but Keem decided to spare him. I didn't get into details with him because that opened my eyes to the functionality of his organization and how it was easily infiltrated. I made sure that nigga Charvo knew he'd be seeing me soon; I needed Kaila in my life whether the nigga was going to accept it or not.

CHAPTER TWELVE

CHARVO HARRIS

L ying in bed with my eyes shut as tight as possible, I tried to keep my breathing steady while Kaila maneuvered through our bedroom as she dressed. I had been sleeping on the couch since I got back in town, but last night, I got tired of sleeping alone, so I crept into bed with her. She had the comforter wrapped tightly around her body as if that was going to stop me from cuddling next to her. When she felt me trying to get under the blanket with her, she reached over and started smacking me, and I winced in pain with each blow. She knew I was fucked up right now, and the pain I experienced daily was enough to make a grown-ass man weak in the knees.

Kaila tried to force me out of bed, but when she saw I wasn't budging, she snatched the blanket and pillows and left the room. With a smile on my face, sleep came easily. She would have to get used to us being back on good terms. She probably thought this was over between us, but I planned to get back in her good graces. All I needed was a little more time.

"Charvo." She kicked the side of the bed to wake me, and I stirred slowly as if I was just now waking up.

"What's up, baby? Where are you headed to looking good like that?"

"Cut the shit, Charvo. Where did you put my keys and purse? It was on the counter in the kitchen, but now it's not there. I need my stuff so I can get the kids to school on time."

"I didn't touch your stuff, Kaila. I ate dinner and then went to sleep like I do every night. Go ask the kids. You know they are always touching stuff they shouldn't touch."

"The kids know not to touch my purse and keys. Charvo, please get the fuck up and get my stuff. You're acting childish as fuck, and I don't have time for it."

"Kaila, I already told you I don't know where it is. The only other option is for me to drop y'all off. I'll throw on some clothes, and we can take the kids to school and then grab breakfast. Give me a few minutes," I told her as I took my time getting out of bed.

My body was still achy, but I felt much better than I had a week ago.

I quickly brushed my teeth and relieved my bladder before throwing on a T-shirt and sweatpants. Moving as fast as my body would allow, I walked outside to see Kaila and the kids standing next to her old Altima, waiting to be let in.

My Camaro sat in the driveway after getting out of the shop two days prior. I had to come out of pocket with almost seven thousand dollars to get the Camaro repainted and repaired; the body damage was extensive, and the entire fuel system had to be replaced. I hadn't figured out who laid hands on my shit yet, but when I did, I'd make sure they reimbursed me for the unnecessary money I had to spend.

As a family, we headed to the school, which put me in a great mood. I listened as Kaila ran through her morning routine with them, ensuring all homework was completed and that all documents requiring a signature were signed. I admired her for being a great mother to our children; she constantly sacrificed to ensure they were comfortable. I could admit that I had fallen short when it came to being the father they needed me to be, but my father didn't even live in the same household as me growing up, so I knew I was doing more than mine ever did.

"I need to go by my job before we return home," Kaila told me once she got out of the car after dropping the kids off.

Nodding my response, I pulled out of the pickup line, and it only took us twenty minutes to make it to her job. I told her I'd wait for her in the parking lot, but she instructed me to leave and told me that she'd get a ride home.

Instead of listening to her, I decided to park in the closest spot to the building entrance. If she thought getting rid of me would be that easy, she'd better think again.

"Charvo, what the fuck is your problem? Look at my purse and keys. I swear to God, I fucking hate your stupid ass."

Wiping the sleep from my eyes, I looked around in temporary confusion, trying to figure out where I was. Quickly realizing I had fallen asleep in the parking lot at her job, I raised the driver's seat to get myself under control.

Kaila had the back door open as she pulled out her purse from under the passenger seat where I had stuffed it last night to force her to ride with me.

"How did that get under there?" I quipped.

"You know precisely how, Charvo. I had the bright idea to check the location of my AirPods, and wouldn't you know, it pinged to this exact spot. I'm unsure what you don't understand about me and you being over, but I'm done, Charvo. The little games and mind tricks you're trying to play won't work anymore. I've put up with you for years, and I'm tired. Just let me go, Charvo. Please let me go."

"I love you, Kaila. I want us to work. A nigga is out here

trying to walk the straight and narrow, but you're making this shit hard. I can admit I fucked up, but I'm doing right by you now, Kaila. I swear I haven't touched another bitch. I'm not texting or calling anyone else... I'm just focusing on you and the kids."

"We're outside my job right now, beating a dead horse. A week ago, we were in Orlando, and you had the bitch who was supposed to be my fucking sister and best friend up there too! So, tell me, what am I making difficult? I haven't even begun to put the pieces together to figure out how long you've been fucking that grimy-ass bitch, but when I do take the time to figure it out, both you and her will have to see me. Have a good fucking day." She slammed the door so hard I thought the glass would shatter.

Kaila got into the back seat of a waiting Uber, and the car quickly pulled out of the lot. Throwing the truck in drive, I hit the gas to speed out of the lot, but my truck didn't move. Looking down to make sure the gear was in drive, I noticed the emergency brake had been engaged, giving Kaila's slick ass just enough time to get away from me.

Peeling out of her job lot, I sped in the direction the Uber went, hoping to see them. Coming to a red light, there were a few cars ahead of me, but from my position, I couldn't tell if it was the same car.

As soon as the light changed, one of the cars cut off a few people to get through traffic, and I knew it had to be her telling the driver to get out of the area as quickly as they could. Knowing all the side streets in Miami, I cut through traffic and hit a quick right turn. Flying through the stop signs at the corner of each street, I whipped left and was back on the main road at another red light. Looking left and then right, I only saw the Uber taillights as the drawbridge signal began to light up. Smashing my foot down on the gas, I went from zero to sixty in seven seconds and beat the lowering rails blocking traffic for the bridge to rise.

When I reached the other side, the car was long gone. I was beating myself up for letting her get away. My phone began to ring over the truck's Bluetooth system.

"What you want, Ann?"

"Charvo, my car just broke down on the way to urgent care with my granny. Come pick us up. We're at the RaceTrac on 119th. Can you hurry up? I don't want her to catch a heat stroke out here."

"If it's an emergency, call the ambulance, Ann. I'm handling business right now and nowhere near that side of town."

"Are you serious, Charvo? I do have your location, and I see that you're less than ten minutes away. Can you please stop playing and come? I never ask you for shit. This is the least you could do for me."

"Location? Aight, give me a few," I said, ending the call and going into the Find My application on my phone.

Kaila and I used to share locations a while ago. Although I stopped sharing mine with her, I didn't think she ever stopped sharing hers with me.

"Bingo!" I smiled like a Cheshire Cat. Her location showed she was two miles away from me, and the dot wasn't moving. Tapping the icon to go to her location, I followed the GPS until I arrived at a luxury apartment complex.

I figured the nigga she had been fucking around on me with had a little bit of money, but I thought he would at least own a house or something. That nigga must've been out here broke hustling just like me. I chuckled to myself.

I parked in one of the first open spaces and called Kaila until she answered the phone.

"If I were you, I would walk out of that nigga's apartment

before I go through this whole complex and start kicking doors down until I find you."

"Charvo, go find something safe to do. You're in my business now, and we don't need that." Kaila laughed in my ear.

Squeezing my phone, wishing it was her face, the call ended before I could speak again.

I had a trick for her ass. I started smashing down on the horn and driving through the complex to gain the attention of all the nosey-ass residents. Since it was midday, I knew most people should've been at work. I saw a buff nigga with long dreads emerge from what looked like the rental office at the center of the complex, and he flagged me down to get my attention.

"Are you lost or looking for somebody?" the man asked as my window went down.

"My girl is over here somewhere with a nigga. You know how this shit goes. Just a family feud. Don't mean to disturb anything."

"Well, you're disturbing everything right about now. I suggest you get the fuck out of here and deal with your issues somewhere else."

"I'm not leaving until my wife comes out," I said before blaring my truck's horn.

The man walked off with a head nod. I shot him a middle finger as I laughed.

Not focusing on the road, my truck came to an abrupt halt from crashing into something. Looking up at the driver in the other vehicle, my eyes landed on the same nigga who was responsible for me only being able to see clearly out of one eye.

The nigga was out of his truck and mobbing over to mine. I didn't even think to lock the doors as he opened my driver's door and snatched me out of the seat.

"Didn't I tell you to keep your ass out of my motherfucking

city, nigga?" He had me jacked up against my truck. Looking past him with my good eye, I saw the taller nigga who stopped me a little while ago walking toward me with a pistol in his hand.

"You know this nigga, Tyree?"

"Nah... I don't."

"Nigga, you fucking my bitch! You know exactly who the fuck I am," I spat.

He sent a quick punch to my rib cage, and unbearable pain coursed through my body. He hit me in the same spot he kicked me in with some thick-ass steel-toe boots a week ago.

I was struggling to stay on my feet as I held my aching rib cage. Kaila came rushing out of the rental office with another chick following closely behind her.

"Charvo, come on, man. Are you serious right now? I told you to leave me alone. We're done. I'm doing what I have to do to get out of your life."

"You gon stand there and let this nigga handle me like this, Kaila? You're supposed to be my bottom bitch, my ride or die. These niggas out here trying to kill me, and you're just standing there, watching the shit go down."

"Because I told you to leave me alone! We don't have to be on bad terms. When you had me, you fucked me over. Please get in your truck and leave. We can talk at the house when I get there with the kids."

"At the house? You know what, since you're putting this nigga before me and the kids, you can have him! You will never see my kids again, bitch. Fuck you and this fuck—"

The nigga stepped back and punched me in the face one good time. My nose twisted as the slow trickle of blood turned into a steady stream. The niggas stepped back to let me leave. Using the last bit of strength I had, I turned to Kaila and spit in her face before hopping in my truck and getting the fuck out of there.

"If you think I'm going to keep sitting in this house with all these kids, you really got me messed up, Charvo. Get here now! They are all crying about being hungry. I have a damn headache, and I need to make a few runs myself."

"When I called you to come over, you said it was no problem. Why are you complaining now? I have moves to make and hella mouths to feed. Get in the kitchen and make a big ass pot of noodles or something. As much as you be on your phone, yo' ass needs to scroll and find a damn recipe you can throw together. Eating out every day is a waste of money."

"Money that you don't do anything with, Charvo. I don't like this switching-up shit you've been doing on me since Kaila left your ass. Any time I've needed money in the past, you came through without thinking twice. What's so different now? All these years, you said you would choose me when the opportunity presented itself. Now that the cat is out of the bag, we can be all about each other, care for these kids, and start our legacy."

"Man, you trippin'. I ain't never said no shit like that to you. Get the fuck off my phone. I'll get at you later."

Stuffing my phone into my back pocket as I walked inside my aunt's house, I greeted my uncle, who was in the living room watching football highlights, and continued on to the kitchen, where I heard my mom and aunt talking.

I was hopeful that they would've gotten a phone call by now about Green's body being found, but I hadn't heard anything yet, so I was over there to figure out what the fuck was going on with that nigga.

"The fact that you've been running around my city thinking you're invincible is wild to me. Dade County usually breeds some stand-up niggas, yet you're out here folding quicker than a lawn chair. I have one question for you. Was it the bitch in your blood that made you walk away from this nigga, not knowing if he was dead or alive?"

Green's dark eyes stared a hole through my soul when I entered the dark room and saw him staring at me. He had all kinds of tubes and breathing devices connected to his body. Chills ran down my spine, causing the tiny hairs all over my body to rise. I thought the nigga was dead.

"This is exactly how I know you niggas aren't built for this business. How the fuck y'all let a bitch... my bitch get the drop on you niggas?"

The distinct sound of high heels clicking against a floor grew louder by the second. When the person finally reached the door, I was shocked to see Alexia standing there with a smirk.

"I heard you niggas were looking for me." She snickered.

"Damn," I mumbled, shaking my head at the sight of her.

Alexia and I had hit many licks together over the years. If someone had told me that she would be the one to double-cross me, I would've killed them right where they stood.

"I warned you a long time ago about keeping it a buck with me, Charvo. I ran the numbers, baby, and I'm sad you've been shorting me on every single drop we made together. According to my calculations, you owe me close to seven hundred thousand, and I'm here to collect."

"Hold on now, beauty. We will handle that but let us finish talking business for a minute," the fat nigga Keem instructed her. She kissed him a few times, and he smacked her on the ass as she walked out of the room.

"Make his bitch ass stand up," I heard someone say before stepping out of the shadows.

It was the nigga who had me on FaceTime earlier.

"I don't know what type of clown ass show you niggas call yourselves running, but we ain't got time for this. If you're going to kill me, do that shit right now and look me in my eyes. If that ain't why I'm here, respectfully, I can see myself out. Y'all got what y'all came for, so it ain't no reason for me even to be caught up in all this. That nigga was the one who stole from you, and obviously, your bitch got it back. If you let me walk away right now, we ain't gon' have any further issues. I promise you that."

"You like to put your hands on your baby mama?" The nigga stepped to my face with balled fists as he stared down at me. He towered over me by a few inches, but I was still a man about mine. I'd never let another nigga hoe me.

"The last thing you should be worried about is what I do with my hoes. If we're talking business, she ain't got shit to do with this." I scoffed, looking the man in his eyes.

"It's a simple yes or no. All that extra shit ain't necessary."

"And if it's a yes..."

I swallowed my words as his fists pummeled my face until I was knocked off my feet. His big construction boots stomped and kicked every part of my body.

"Put me out of my fucking misery!" I yelled, spitting out blood and a few cracked teeth.

"Nah, nigga, fight back. This is how you do Kaila, right?" One more hard kick to the face, and my eyes landed on Green. The nigga was tickled pink at the sight of me getting my ass beat. I bet he wished he could've gotten up and finished me off.

Fuck you, I mouthed the words directly at Green before one last blow to the side of my head caused me to black out.

"What are y'all in here gossiping about?" Entering the kitchen, I kissed my mom and aunt before sitting at the dining room table across from them.

"What the hell happened to you?" my aunt questioned as they both stared at me, surveying the visible damage.

"Got into a little scuffle last week, had to piece a lil nigga up, but it's all good. I came by to see if you heard from Green, Auntie. He still hasn't hit me up, and I've been calling him for a week now."

"You know that cousin of yours. I believe he texted me a couple of days ago, or maybe I read the message late, but I'm sure he's running around this damn state somewhere. He can never sit his ass still. That's why them knuckleheaded thugs are always shooting my shit up."

"That's crazy. Maybe it's time for you to relocate. There are plenty of places you can move to so you can be off the radar until he shows face again. Green has the whole state searching high and low for him. Ain't no telling how bad it could get the next time someone comes looking for him."

"I'm not going anywhere. They would've made it happen a long time ago if they wanted me gone, nephew." She waved me off.

"Aight, I guess I'll be getting out of here. Ann is at the house with all the kids, and she keeps calling me. Do you mind if I take some of this food home? Or if you have leftovers, I can take them. She doesn't know how to cook, and I'm tired of buying fast food and shit. My kids shouldn't be eating that every night."

"Go in the fridge and take all of that. I made it yesterday and lost my appetite when I finished cooking. Your uncle can't eat as much of that stuff anymore, so it'll go to waste if nobody else takes it."

My mom helped me make to-go plates for me to take

home. She loaded each one up and opened the front door for me to leave.

"How you doing, Auntie? Nice to see my little cousin checking on my people." The sight of Green sitting on a rocking chair on the porch made me piss my pants and drop the bags of food I'd been holding. "We gotta talk business nigga. Have a seat."

CHAPTER THIRTEEN

KAILA MOFFETT

"Why do we have to keep meeting like this, Kaila? If you would give me your number, we could set up a time to meet that's most convenient for both of us." Tyree was leaning against my truck outside the apartment rental office when I walked out.

I'd moved into the apartment over the weekend with an air mattress, blanket, toothpaste, and a pack of toilet paper since Charvo was still being a bitch about me going to the house to get my stuff and pick up the kids. All he wanted to talk about was me fucking on another nigga and abandoning my family, and I was honestly tired of the argument. I missed my kids more than words could express, but I was struggling to come up with a game plan to get them without Charvo knowing.

"That sounds good, but I'm cool. I'm focusing on myself right now. I'll keep you in mind when I am ready."

"Keeping me in mind is sweet but not enough for me because I can't get you off mine." He licked his lips, and I quickly diverted my eyes, remembering our time in Orlando.

We had a few close encounters, but I managed to maintain my self-control.

"Why do you keep popping up here whenever I come to the office?"

"A little birdie sends out the bat signal, and then I suit up and come running. If I had your number, though, we could sit down for a meal, and you could give me a tour of your new spot—you know, the things that normal people do when they're trying to build up to something."

"That would be amazing if only we were building up to something. I have to go, Tyree. My baby daddy is still not letting me see my kids because he thinks we have something going on, so I'm trying to beat him to the pickup line today."

"Why do you continue putting up with him, Kaila? From the short time we spent together, I can tell you're a great woman with a nice head on your shoulders, and you're a damn good mother. You know he only keeps those kids away from you because that's the easiest way to hurt you?"

"I know, but what can I do at this point? I put all my savings into getting this apartment, and now I need to sign up for school, plus the holidays are coming up. It's a lot on me, and I'm just trying to keep my head above water right now."

"You're talking to a man right now, mama. The majority of those problems can be eliminated if you allow me to show you what I can do. I'm not here to give you a handout; it's more of a hand-up. You can ask both of my baby's moms, I'm not typically the kind of nigga who goes out of his way to do a bunch of sweet and romantic shit, but it's something about you that I don't want to live without, Kaila Moffett. I like you... a lot." With little effort, Tyree pulled my body forward until we collided.

This man was too damn good to be true, and after everything I'd gone through with Charvo, I refused to let another man take charge of my heart just to break it.

"Tyree, I'm sorry. I just can't right now. I want you—I mean, I want to focus on getting myself together without a man. I've wasted the last few years of my life with one I thought I would have a fairytale ending with, and you were a direct witness of how that ended."

"I hear you, and I respect that, Kaila. Just know I'm right here. You got my nose wide open; I'm locked in on you."

"I appreciate you," I responded, and he leaned forward, giving me forehead kisses. This man knew how to make my heart melt, and he really didn't even know me.

"What were you saying about getting the kids? Let's go back to that." He switched the conversation and released the light hold he had on me so I could create space between us, but my body refused to move away from his. Something about him felt like home to me.

"I have to beat Charvo to the pick-up line. If I can get them first, he doesn't have a choice but to let them come back here with me. We don't have a custody agreement in place, so the police can't make me give them back to him if they do come over here."

"Why don't we just go to the courthouse and file an emergency custody order? I know a few people who can pull some strings to have something in place by the time the sun sets."

"I don't have the money to file anything right now." I was embarrassed about my financial situation because I literally had to spend what was left in all my accounts except my emergency fund to secure the apartment.

Although I didn't have to pay the first month's rent, the double security deposit, light bill deposit, internet set up, and the small grocery shopping I'd managed to do still put a hurting on my pockets. I still had a task list of other things I needed to buy for the kids, but I planned to make it work with whatever I could scrape up until I got paid at the end of the week.

"Aight, I know you want to make it to the school to get the kids, but I'm uncomfortable letting you leave like this. If I promise I can handle this for you, will you let me help you through this?"

I struggled with letting a man lead because every single time I let go of the wheel and let Charvo take control, he drove us straight to hell. Tyree's pleading eyes were more than enough promise that he could single-handedly fix my current predicament, but my mind still told me to say no.

"Just give me this one chance, Kaila. I ain't no begging ass nigga, but if you want me to get down on my knees right now, I will." He was about to drop to the sidewalk before I quickly stopped him.

"The last time a man got down on one knee for me, it didn't end well. I'll give you this chance, Tyree. Please don't mess this up."

"I got you, mama. I want you to park in your spot and come ride with me. I foresee a Target run on the agenda, and I'm almost sure I have more space in the truck's bed than you do in your trunk."

Doing as he instructed without putting up any more of a fight, I backed into my spot and secured the truck before hopping into Tyree's Dodge Ram.

The smooth R&B playlist he had in rotation helped ease my mind as we headed to the courthouse. On the way there, Tyree made a few phone calls to ensure the right people awaited us upon our arrival. I enjoyed watching him switch up his lingo from street to professional; that told me that he was one of those niggas who knew how to handle business when it was time.

As promised, we were in and out of the courthouse in less than two hours, and I walked out with a temporary full custody agreement for my children. I did have to provide proof that they were currently living in unsafe conditions at the house, which included pictures I kept in a hidden folder of all the times Charvo had left bruises and marks on my body after he put his hands on me. That was something I wished Tyree had never seen, but there was no way for me to hide it. I wondered if it made him think differently of me or if he thought I was weak for letting a man lay his hands on me.

"When it's time for us to pick them up, the police will be there with us to avoid any commotion on his end. Are the kids' rooms set up already, or do we need to grab a few things for them?"

"I was going to give them the air mattress to sleep on for a few days. We'll be okay," I assured him as I glanced over the documents in my hands. I didn't realize he had stopped walking until I made it to the truck and noticed he wasn't beside me.

"That was a yes or no question, mama."

"No... the rooms aren't set up."

"That's all I needed from you. You'll get the hang of this sooner than later." Tyree stepped around me and opened the door so I could get into his truck before walking around to the driver's seat. I wasn't sure where our next destination would be, but I was more than ready for the ride.

When most men bragged about being the king of their cities, they were talking out the side of their necks. But when Tyree Roman claimed that title, it was all action behind those words. At exactly 6:07 PM, the last of the furniture deliveries were brought inside my apartment to be set up. The kitchen pantry was over-flowing with enough food and drinks to last us for a while.

Every time I tried to thank Tyree for everything he'd done for me, he walked off to see what else he could help put together before we went to pick up the kids.

My nerves were all over the place just thinking about the task. Knowing Charvo, he'd put on a show for anyone willing to watch his antics. After our exchange outside the rental office, I blocked his number and email address to prevent him from contacting me. He only wanted to talk about fixing our family and giving us another chance; I was tired of it.

"My guy won't be able to mount the televisions until tomorrow afternoon. Besides that, everything in the bedrooms is set up and ready for use. Do we need to make any more stops before picking up your kids?" Tyree slipped off his shirt, exposing the ink covering his upper torso.

Like staring at a starry night sky, I was entranced by the detailed work and wanted to know every detail about each tattoo.

"Y... yes," I stammered.

Tyree stepped into my space, and the scent of Dolce and Gabbana Light Blue invaded my nostrils. I quickly shook away the thoughts that started running wild in my mind. "I'm sorry. It was such a busy day that I didn't eat anything, so I'm a little lethargic."

"Let's feed you before we pick them up. I'm sure they are going to want all your attention." This man had me so wrapped up in his trance that I couldn't even think for myself in his presence.

When the last of the setup crew left my apartment, Tyree and I followed them out.

"What do you like to eat?" Tyree asked once he got in the truck after opening my door for me.

"I'll take a salad. It's already after eight," I remarked, and Tyree slammed on the brakes in the middle of a busy street. The car behind us sounded its horn and quickly drove around us, flipping Tyree off.

"You haven't eaten anything all day. A salad isn't going to cut it, Kaila. Please don't ever try your life like that again."

"I don't need to eat anything heavy since it's already late in the day. I don't need to do anything to gain any more weight," I mumbled.

"What's wrong with your weight?"

"Can you drive, please? All these cars keep shooting us looks since you are literally blocking traffic."

"What's wrong with your weight, Kaila Moffett?"

"Don't act like you can't see that I'm a big girl, Tyree. I could miss a few meals." I frowned.

"Whoever put that in your head as a negative attribute can talk to me about that. Ain't nothing wrong with a woman who has some weight on her. You look good as fuck, and don't ever let anyone tell you differently. Now, tell me what you want to eat so I can stop blocking traffic." He smirked at me.

"It's a Dutch Pot not too far from here. I'll have some oxtail."

"Shit, that sounds good to me."

As Tyree drove, we had light conversations that flowed easily. From our initial weekend in Orlando, I knew he was an amazing man. His children's mothers spoke highly of him, and I was impressed by the dynamic of their family unit. Tyree was serious about keeping every aspect of his life in order. I pictured myself as an extension of their cohesive unit for a moment, but I quickly let go of those thoughts. I had too much going on in my personal life to try to fit into theirs.

"The sheriff is sitting outside the house, so he'll be ready to serve Charvo and get the kids out of the house. Let's pray it goes as smoothly as possible."

"I don't have a good feeling about this. Charvo is going to make a scene; that's his character. I don't want the kids to have to witness any of this."

"As long as we think positive, we'll always have positive outcomes. I'm right here with you through all of this." Tyree reached over and gripped my thigh to remind me of his presence.

Before we arrived at the house to pick up the kids, we stopped at Munchy's Pizza to get a pie, wings, garlic rolls, and soda. My anxiety steadily increased as we got closer to the house.

When we got out of the truck, the police officer greeted us and led the way to the front door. I didn't see Charvo's truck in the driveway, but there were lights on all over the house, so we knew someone was there.

Officer Randle knocked on the door, stepped back, and paced a bit.

"No, don't go to the door. My mama always told us not to open the door if we are home alone." I knew that was Taika's voice coming from inside.

"Home alone?" I stepped toward the door and knocked again.

"Taika, it's me, baby girl. Walk over to the window so you can see me, and then open the door."

"I told you it's Mommy," Cadell loved to argue with his sister like he was her damn daddy.

The moment the front door opened, all three of my kids rushed out to hug me. Since the days each of them came on this earth, I had never been away from them, and Charvo knew that. Whenever he wanted to hurt me, he knew anything involving my kids would break me to the core.

"Where is your daddy? Are you really home alone?" I asked after carefully looking each of them over.

"Auntie Pepper was here, but she told us she was coming right back. Daddy hasn't been here since yesterday, I think," Taika explained.

Wiping my face with my hand as I released a deep breath, I reserved all my comments and went inside to begin packing our belongings.

"I need you to grab the suitcases out of the closet and take your clothes, shoes, and any toys you want to take. We have a new house that's ready for all of us to move into. Please make sure you have underwear and socks, too. Does everybody understand me?"

My children nodded their heads in unison before rushing off to do as instructed.

I asked Tyree to help the boys, especially because I knew how easily they could get distracted.

"Hi, Auntie Kaila." Penny and Caiden ran up and hugged me just as I was about to enter the bedroom.

"Hey, y'all. What are y'all doing here?" I asked, kneeling down to speak to Pepperann's children.

"We live here with you now. Mommy is going to get us some food. She should be back soon."

"You live here now?" I repeated the phrase, looking back and forth between them. When they confirmed, I instructed them to sit and watch TV, then proceeded to the bedroom.

The door was wide open, and the sight of the room instantly pissed me off. The walls used to display pictures of Charvo, me, and the kids and photos of my pregnancies. I also had a small memorial on my side of the room dedicated to my parents and godmother, but all of it was gone. A stranger wouldn't even believe I ever lived in that house.

Instead of looking through the bedroom to find my stuff, I set my pride aside and called Charvo.

"What's good, baby? I was thinking about you."

"Cut the shit, Charvo. You moved this bitch and her kids in the house and got rid of my stuff?"

"Huh? What bitch, Kaila? Where are you right now? I can pull up on you so we can talk."

"I'm at the fucking house to get my kids and my stuff, but it's not here! I swear to God, if you or that bitch threw away my stuff, I'm setting this fucking house on fire with y'all in it."

Tyree rushed into the bedroom to see what was going on with me after hearing the one-sided conversation. I was so fucking tired of crying over this situation, but I knew it was tears of anger falling this time around. I had given this nigga nine years of my life that I would never be able to get back, and now I was left with nothing. This was the type of shit that made a bitch smile in her mugshot.

"Who's in my room? I told y'all badasses to stay out of that room!"

Tyree couldn't get a grip on me as I sprinted out the door.

Pepperann turned her head in my direction and was abruptly met with a slap to the face, knocking her into the wall. "All this fucking time, I should've known you were a snake-ass bitch, Pepper! If you wanted my life that bad, all you had to do was ask for it. You and that grimy ass nigga are made for each other, bitch." With an open hand, I smacked the wig off her fucking head before Tyree got between us.

"You know I'm good with Officer Randle, but we don't need him coming in here right now. He has to deal with the kids being left alone, so I need you to chill out, mama. Look at me, Kaila," he commanded.

I was fuming mad, my fists clenched, and I couldn't stop pacing the floor. I wanted to beat the snot out of Pepperann for playing in my fucking face. I called that bitch my sister, and this was how she did me.

"She gotta feel me, Tyree. I looked out for this bitch on multiple occasions when I didn't have a dime to my fucking name. I was the one who threw the baby showers for her kids... hell, I named her first kid. I swear to God, she gotta feel me."

"I hear you, Kaila, but now isn't the time. Let's see if she knows where your stuff is so we can get out of here. I'm not about to let you lose yourself behind this. Her time will come, just like the time will come for your baby daddy to see me. We're good, Kaila. I promise we'll handle them."

"Where the fuck is my stuff? All my pictures, the memorial for my parents, clothes, shoes, and documents. Where is our stuff, Pepperann?"

"Charvo put it in the storage out back." She sniffled.

"I don't know why you're crying. You're getting what you wanted, right?" Stepping over her, Tyree was on my ass as I walked out the back door to get into the storage.

All my belongings were neatly packaged in the outdoor storage room, which made it quick and easy for Tyree to load everything into his truck. As he was grabbing the last of everything and I got the kids into the car, Charvo's truck was blazing down the road with his music blasting. He stopped his truck directly in front of Tyree's and hopped out with his gun aimed at Tyree. He winced in pain as he stepped down wrong on his ankle, which was still healing from the ass-whooping he had taken a few weeks ago, but he did his best to bite back the pain.

"What the fuck you doing at my house, fuck nigga? Get them the fuck out of this raggedy ass truck, Kaila. My kids ain't going nowhere with this nigga."

The fact that he drew his weapon when the police cruisers

were clearly visible in front of his house told me that he had been binge drinking and he wasn't worried about the consequences of his actions. Everyone could smell the liquor oozing out of his pores as he swayed with every small gust of wind.

Officer Randle and another police officer who had arrived at the scene had their weapons drawn the moment Charvo hopped out of his truck. Tyree remained cool, calm, and collected as he instructed me to get into the truck.

"Put the weapon down, sir! This is your only warning. There are women and children out here, and we don't want anyone getting hurt. Drop the weapon!"

His glossed-over eyes blinked a few times as if that would help him sober up.

"Why is she taking my kids? I just wanted to love her, but she doesn't love me anymore," Charvo cried, dropping to his knees, and the gun slipped out of his hand.

Officer Randle tackled him to the ground as his partner kicked the weapon away. This was the last thing I wanted the kids to see; this was my biggest fear.

CHAPTER FOURTEEN

TYREE ROMAN

P ulling into the valet line outside the Brazilian steakhouse, I adjusted the collar on my shirt and took one last look in the rearview mirror to ensure my fresh lineup was still crisp. Since Vanessa, Starja, and the kids made it back to town from their week-long cruise, she had decided it was time to schedule a sit-down with me and her new man. Her favorite restaurant, Chima, was in Fort Lauderdale, so I left an hour and a half ahead of our meet-up time to beat the traffic. Although Miami and Fort Lauderdale were a short distance from each other, the traffic was sometimes unbearable.

"Appreciate you," I told the valet attendant as I stepped out of my white-on-black Maserati. This was one of the cars I pulled out when I wanted to stunt a little bit. The thick Cuban link bracelets and pinky ring added just enough to make the all-black attire I wore look like some shit out of a magazine. I rarely got the opportunity to step out, but when I did, I knew how to put some shit together.

When I gave her my name, the hostess walked me into a private room. Vanessa's only instructions were to make sure we met in a private space. I didn't like too many listening ears, so it was a must that we kept shit low-key.

Entering the room, Starja was already seated and sipping a glass of red wine while scrolling through her phone.

"Look at you. I almost want to tell you to take me home with you tonight," Starja flirted as she greeted me with a hug.

"Sounds good, but we know it ain't been that kind of party in years," I reminded her.

Respecting the mothers of my children was always at the top of my priority list. Since I never committed myself to a relationship with either of them, I never felt the need to play house or slide up in them whenever I felt like it. Our dynamic was strictly focused on the kids and their well-being, and over the last few years, we'd managed to keep it that way.

When Vanessa found out about my baby with Starja, she came at me sideways about a relationship and wanted more from me than I could give her at the time, but I had to explain to her that I didn't want what she wanted from me. I remembered the days when they bumped heads at the sight of each other. I'd have to pick up one kid at Walmart and then drive thirty minutes out of my way to pick up the other one. A few years ago, I got caught up in some street shit that had me lying low for a few months, and that's what it took for them to get on the same page. I hated that it took me to almost lose my life for them to see how important it was for all of us to get along, but I was thankful it finally happened.

I made a vow to them both that I would ensure they were taken care of as long as there was breath in my body since they gave me the greatest gifts a man could ask for. And to this day, I'd remained true to my word. If they never wanted to work again, I'd handle that, but both of them were too independent for a nigga like me to convince them to stay in the house.

"Yeah, don't even remind me." Starja rolled her eyes.

"Speaking of taking somebody home, I didn't have a chance to thank you for allowing me to take over the house. It's been a rocky couple of months trying to get everything closed out with my old vendor while trying to find a new one, but I know it will get better soon."

"Why didn't you tell me you were having problems, Starja? You know I could've handled that."

"Because I needed to fix this on my own. If I run to you for every little inconvenience, I'd be relying on you for the rest of my life. I know you don't mind, but I do, Tyree. I want to be financially stable whether I have you or not."

"I understand that, but I'd rather you come to me instead of struggling in silence. We're family, Starja, and we will always be that. Your well-being is just as important as Shariyah's. If you're okay, I know she's okay. If you need anything else, please let me know. I can shoot you the bread, make some phone calls, or do whatever I have to do to help."

"I heard you, Tyree, and I appreciate you. Things will be fine soon. My trip is coming up, so we'll talk when I return. I've been considering expanding into a new industry, but I'm still putting my feelers out."

"See, that hustle right there is what you get from me," I joked, lightening the mood in the room.

"Hey, y'all!" The door opened, Vanessa walked in first, and her date came right behind her.

"Starja and Tyree, this is—"

"Jaxson," we said simultaneously.

"My motherfucking nigga Jaxson!"

"Tyree! Long time no see, brother. How the heck have you been?" Jaxson and I slapped hands before pulling each other into a brotherly hug. Technically, Jaxson wasn't a nigga, but this white boy ran the streets with us years ago, and he had always been a solid ass dude.

"Shit, I've been cooling, man, raising these kids and keeping these two as stress-free as possible."

"I hear you, dude. Man, it's been years. It's such a small world."

Vanessa and Starja stared at us as we took a quick trip down memory lane until we realized they were staring.

"I'm sorry, baby. Let me get that for you," Jaxson told Vanessa as he pulled a chair out for her to sit.

"It is a small world," I remarked, sitting down across from them.

"Since it seems like you two know each other, I just want to put a disclaimer out there and let you know that I didn't know him from a can of paint when we met," Vanessa gushed as she stared into his eyes.

Jaxson was one of those white boys who you knew grew up in the hood. He was never ashamed or embarrassed about where he came from.

Jaxson was the first one to move out of the hood when we were coming up, and he went off to the military for a few years. I didn't do too well at keeping up with people from my younger years, so seeing him doing well for himself was refreshing.

"How did y'all meet? Y'all look so good together. You compliment her so well, Jaxson," Starja gushed.

"Do y'all remember when I took that trip to Colorado a few years ago?"

"Uh yes, the same trip I was mad about you not inviting me on. How could I forget?" Starja laughed.

"I actually flew her out. That was our official first date," Jaxson explained. "We met on one of these dating apps and instantly connected. I didn't think she was actually going to get on a plane and travel across the country to meet me, but when she stepped off of that plane and ran to me, that was all it took."

"We stayed in a cabin right in the mountains. Now that I think about it, we should probably plan a family trip during Christmas break this year. I'm sure the kids would love to go skiing," Vanessa said, and Starja ate it all up.

I rarely planned our family vacations, so wherever they told me they wanted to go, I just needed the dates, and I'd be there.

The waitress entered the room to take drink orders and review the protocol for our dining experience. I hadn't eaten since breakfast this morning, so I planned to smash all the lamb chops and well-done steaks my stomach could handle. When she left, the ladies headed off to get their sides from the buffet-style setup, leaving Jaxson and me alone in the private room.

"I heard you got out sometime last year. How has that been for you?" Jaxson inquired as soon as the door closed. We could see out of the glass panels that lined the walls of the room, but people on the outside couldn't look in. So, I kept my eyes on the ladies.

"It's been cool. Honestly, I feel like I'm finally in a good space. Spending more time with the kids and focusing on the things I had to neglect while running that business. You know how that goes."

"I wish I could say the same."

Jaxson's tone forced me to look at him to read his expression. He remained stone-faced as he took intentional sips from the cognac in his glass.

"Didn't you go to the military? I'm sure they're still cutting you a check for that shit. All the benefits people tell me about make me wish I could've done the same thing."

"Shit, I'm sure the benefits are great, but I never got to experience that. A new opportunity arose to the tune of one of our old connections getting popped. I had to do a favor for a favor."

Jaxson speaking in circles and riddles wasn't working for me. I needed the nigga to be direct; I didn't do well with people who beat around the bush.

"The whole hood said you went to serve. Do you remember Brian? He said he saw the people in uniforms go to your house at three in the morning and pull you out of bed. That nigga was lying?"

Jaxson unlocked his phone and tapped around before passing it to me.

"Oh shit!" I exclaimed, looking at a picture of Jaxson and Brian standing in front of a multimillion-dollar mansion. "Where the hell is this, and why does this look recent?" I asked, passing his phone back.

"That was last week. We are still getting money together and doing what we have to do."

"I'm happy to hear that." I nodded. "I got out when I felt I'd put in enough time. Plus, the old plug stopped fucking with me over some bullshit, and I was tired of being fucked over. I set my partner Keem up, but now I'm having second thoughts about that. It's been some bullshit going on in his camp. I don't want to tell the nigga what to do, but you know how it goes."

"Oh, I know your boy Keem very well. We *used* to do business together. I made a few dollars off him." The emphasis on his words put my brain to work. Keem never mentioned testing out a new plug, and I knew I didn't make the connection, so I was blindsided by the news.

"How long ago was this?" I was intrigued.

Keem never mentioned working with Jaxson, and I knew Keem knew of him.

"Until about two weeks ago. Found out he was on some snake shit with some kid. His real name is Gerald, but they call him—"

"Green." I finished his statement as the ladies opened the door and entered the room, each carrying two plates.

Jaxson and I switched the conversation to sports, fishing, and reminiscing while my mind danced around thoughts of Keem. He was a solid nigga in my book, and he never gave me a reason to doubt that, but the news Jaxson dropped on me had me running through every fine detail about our last run-in.

As dinner progressed, we all discussed plans for Jaxson to meet the children. The way he adored Vanessa and their evident chemistry showed me that their love for each other was real. I was surprised they had been together for two years already, but she had only recently mentioned wanting to introduce him to us.

"Let me get a second with you, Tyree."

After getting one more drink, the ladies sat in the outdoor seating area while we stepped away from listening ears.

"Seeing as though you brought him in, I want to allow you to rectify this situation. There are people in much higher places than me who've only been letting him make it because of his connection to you."

"I'm not trying to insult your intelligence but spell it out for me, Jax. When I tell you I've been hands-off, I mean that. I tapped in about two weeks ago because he called me when some shit went down, but we took care of that."

"The shit that went down was him and his boy Gerald running off at an exchange to the tune of three hundred racks and enough bricks for the entire east coast."

"So, why the fuck did the nigga have me in Orlando looking for that motherfucker if they were working together?"

"Two snakes intertwined in harmony can't reach success together."

"You fucked me up with this one, Jax. I can't hold you."

"Honestly, I didn't want to bring it to you under these

circumstances, but I couldn't call myself a friend if I stayed silent."

"I know how it goes. How much time do I have?"

"A couple of weeks at most. I'll do what I can to hold them off, but a lot of this is beyond me now."

Shaking hands like business partners, I vowed to Jaxson that I would do my best to get this shit situated, but I had a feeling that this would end in bloodshed and severed ties.

Spring: Kaila asked for your number. Can I give it to her?

Me: About damn time! Hell yeah. You should've been gave it to her.

I smiled at the thought of finally wearing Kaila down. It had been three weeks of me being her Superman, and I didn't plan to let up anytime soon. Since she'd moved into the apartment, I had stopped by twice to make sure everything was good with her and to ensure the contractors I hired to mount the TVs and change the light fixtures got everything done correctly.

As much as I wanted to pop by there every day to see her face, I knew it was best for me to fall back. She was clear about her intentions of not wanting a relationship right now and focusing on herself, so I would respect her wishes.

My phone rang a few minutes later as I pulled into the Target parking lot.

"Why did it take you so long to ask for my number?"

"I'm sorry. I must've dialed the wrong one because you're talking to me like you're my daddy, and he died a long time ago."

"Kaila, quit playing, mama. How are you? I'm happy to finally hear your voice over the phone."

"I'm good, Tyree. I'm making dinner now and was wondering if you wanted a plate. I don't want the leftovers to go to waste."

"I can be there in an hour or so. I have to make a stop, and then I'll slide up on you."

"Okay, see you when you get here."

"What type of wine do you like, Kaila?" I asked before she could hang up.

"I've never had wine before. I'll drink a wine cooler now and then, but that's it."

"I guess it's a first time for everything. I'll see you soon, sweetheart."

The wine aisle was my first stop inside Target. My mom always taught me that a man couldn't go wrong with a fruity bottle of wine for a woman. I grabbed the peach-flavored Stella Rosa, a bouquet of red roses, and a few toys for the kids, then got the other items I came for. I was usually a Walmart kind of nigga, but when Kaila had me in there the other day, I knew I'd be making the change. Damn near every checkout lane was open, and the store was clean; that other store might never see me again.

Kaila must have been watching the Ring camera as I approached her door because she opened it before I knocked.

"A handsome man with two handfuls of Target bags. I almost want to get used to this," she said, opening the door wider for me to step past her.

"Are your kids still up?" I inquired, not hearing any televisions on or kids playing. It was just after 8:00 p.m., but I figured they'd still be up.

"No, they went to bed a few minutes ago. They know I need two hours to myself every night, so they have a set bedtime during the week," she explained.

"I see I'm not the only one who likes to keep things on a set schedule," I joked.

"I'm probably a little more flexible with mine, though," Kaila remarked.

"I got a few things for the kids and one more thing for you in my truck. I'll be right back."

Kaila's hand slipped into mine as I turned to open the door. "Thank you for thinking of the kids. That means a lot to me." Kaila wrapped her arms around my neck as mine slipped around her waist, pulling her body to mine. The soft curves of her body felt perfect to me; I hated that she even thought she needed to change it because of what a fuck nigga put into her head.

Slightly lifting her chin, our lips collided, and what I thought would be a few quick pecks turned into her tongue, which slipped into my mouth to tango with mine. When she pulled back, one of her hands gripped my beard as she pulled my face down for a few more pecks.

"I'll be right back."

I kissed her forehead, and she reluctantly headed into the kitchen while I rushed outside to grab her roses and wine from the truck.

As I approached the back of my truck, I noticed my tailgate was down, and I instantly reached for the Glock tucked into my waistband.

"How the fuck do you go from a bad bitch on your arm, living in one of the most expensive neighborhoods in this city, to a bitch who lives two blocks and a set of train tracks away from the fucking hood, Tyree?" Ashonte sat on the tailgate swinging her legs like she was on a ride at a damn amusement park.

"Ashonte, you almost got your shit popped, fucking with

my truck. What the fuck you got going on? Get off my truck, shawty."

"How about, uhh, no! We need to talk, Tyree, and I'm not going anywhere until we do."

"Well, now is not the fucking time to be talking. You had years to have a big girl conversation with me, but you chose to tuck your tail and suck on an infected bitch's pussy instead. Yeah, you know the streets talking. They loved your little video, but I know that hoe burnt your mouth. That's why you got that little bump right there, right?"

"Ain't nobody burn shit over here, nigga! Whoever your source is, they're unreliable."

"Whatever you say, Ashonte. I gotta go, so take care of yourself and your son."

"If you walk away, I swear to God I'll go kick that bitch's door down right now! I saw you over here helping her fat ass move all that shit into that tiny ass apartment. Was she not good enough for a house? I guess she really ain't me."

"I wouldn't be fucking with her if she was you, Ashonte. I don't even fuck with you. What the hell you doing over here, anyway? Shouldn't you be in jail or somewhere taking care of your jit?"

"I've got lawyers' fees, baby. They couldn't hold me down if they wanted to. I'm over here visiting a friend. We were getting ready to go out when I saw your truck sitting over here. I thought I would come and speak."

"Well, next time, just keep it pushing. I'm going to see about my future wife. Take care of yourself and get the fuck off my truck."

"Fuck this raggedy ass truck." She jumped down from the tailgate. "Like I just said, if we can't talk, I'll go in there with you so we can get to the bottom of all this," Ashonte asserted.

"Get to the bottom of what?"

My heart dropped to my asshole when I heard Kaila's question. Ashonte and I looked at her at the same time.

"You definitely have a type. Big and ugly as fuck!"

"Girl, please cut it out with the elementary school insults. This big and ugly woman will beat you into this concrete. Please don't say shit else to me. Tyree, thank you for coming and everything, but obviously, this was a mistake. Lose my number." Kaila slipped into the darkness as quickly as she came, and when I tried to go after her, Ashonte stepped in my path, snatching the bottle of wine out of my hands, which sent the vase of red roses crashing to the ground.

Ashonte launched the wine bottle in Kaila's direction and stood there like she did her big one. When the glass shattered against the ground, I breathed a sigh of relief that Kaila hadn't been touched.

"You see how easily she walked away? I would've never given up on you like that."

"Man, Ashonte, shut the fuck up. All you do is run your mouth. You don't get tired of talking?" Even though Kaila and I had only just started sparking, I knew that shit had just been put out.

"You're tired of me talking? Well, I have one more thing to tell you, and I'll be out of your way. I'm pregnant, Tyree. We will fix our family whether you like it or not."

CHAPTER FIFTEEN

CHARVO HARRIS

"All it took was that nigga to smile in your face for you to fuck him, huh?"

"Charvo, what are you doing outside of my job? Ain't you supposed to be in jail right now?" Kaila unlocked her truck and set her bags inside.

I had sat outside one of the businesses across the street for two hours, waiting for her to get off. Since she blocked my phone number, I figured she wanted live and in-person FaceTime.

"Lawyer fees, love. I miss you and the kids, Kaila. I'm ready for you to stop playing games and come back home."

"That's not happening, Charvo."

"Why not? Was I really that bad to you? I never thought I'd see the day you gave up on me."

"You gave up on yourself. I stayed down through so much bullshit, Charvo. I really don't have anything left to give you."

"How sway, Kaila, when I've been the one begging for us to get this right since Orlando?"

"How long were you fucking Pepper?" She stared at me

with a blank expression. I was hoping she wouldn't ask about Ann and me, but it was an unrealistic expectation.

"Why do you have to bring her up? She doesn't have anything to do with us."

"This is exactly why I don't want to talk to you. You never keep it real with me, Charvo. Why do you think I haven't let you touch me since March 2020? The only reason I allowed it then is because we were on lockdown, and I was tired of yo' ass complaining about the strip club being closed. This shit between us has been dead, and you're the reason."

"I always keep it real with you, Kaila—"

"How long, Charvo? Since you keep it so real, how long have you been fucking her?"

"I don't know. We were in a bad spot when I met her at the gas station. I know it was fucked up, but it was just some shit that started and went too far. I'm sorry, Kaila. I can end what I have with her so we can focus on our family."

"You can end it? Nigga, it should've never started. Are her kids yours, too?" Sucking my teeth, I sighed loudly at her question.

"That tells me everything I need to know. You take care of yourself, Charvo. My kids need a little time away from you, so during that time, we can figure out a new schedule for you to see them."

"Are you serious, Kaila? I'm not a threat to the kids."

"If my kids can tell me they don't feel safe with you, that's what it is. You didn't do shit when I told you the neighbor pulled a gun out on them, and the bitch you left at the house wasn't feeding them, but she made sure her kids ate. You showed me a long time ago that you didn't care about them, but I looked past all that shit for the sake of our family. That was my mistake. I'll never put another man before my kids. Hard lesson, but I learned it."

"No other man is allowed to be around my kids, Kaila. You're talking about not putting anyone before them when it won't be any of that. If we ain't together, you ain't with nobody!"

"And what the fuck are you going to do to stop me? If I want a nigga to knock my shit loose and then take the kids and me on an all-expenses-paid vacation, I'll fucking do it! You're not about to stand there and tell me what the fuck to do with my life when you've been living yours."

"So, you have been fucking that nigga?"

Running toward her at full speed, I was ready to squeeze the life out of her for playing in my face. I knew she had that lame-ass nigga fucking on her, and that shit probably started when she stopped letting me touch her ass. I was about to snatch her by the locs when a shockwave hit me in the chest and flowed through my body. All my muscles locked up instantly. The electricity flowed from the top of my head to the bottom of my feet, and the sound was deafening. After a few seconds, Kaila stepped back, and my body hit the asphalt like cinderblocks.

"I'm done, Charvo. You will never get another opportunity to put your hands on me, to breathe the same air I breathe, to love, to miss me... none of that shit. The next time you call yourself pulling up at my job to check me, it'll be a bullet waiting with your name on it. Try me if you want to." With a hard kick to my still bruised ribs, Kaila stepped over me, and I heard her truck crank up.

She narrowly missed running me over as she backed out of her parking spot while I was still sprawled on the ground.

I couldn't move for a long time as the effects of the taser were still flowing through me. Kaila and I would have to do this the hard way.

"Do you need me to call the police for you, baby? I saw

everything and recorded it on my phone?" a woman's voice called out to me, but I didn't bother looking around to see where it was coming from. An older lady approached and kneeled down beside me.

"Here, drink this water. I saw what that heifer did to you! She's an evil little thang, I tell you. She tried to get me fired from my job," the woman ranted.

"Who are you? I don't know what you're talking about right now." I grabbed the bottle of water from the woman but looking inside, I saw that the water looked cloudy. I wasn't sure if my eyes were playing tricks on me or if this old woman had slipped something in it, but I wasn't taking a chance.

"I'm her coworker. They put me on unpaid leave, but one of my other good friends called and told me she returned to the office this week. I wanted to pop up on her to give her a piece of my mind for snitching to these white folks on me, but you beat me to her. Don't you worry, though. I got something for her. I've been around a long time, and I know how to handle women like her."

"She's the mother of my children, ma'am. Respectfully, if you do something to her, you won't have to worry about coming to this job anymore."

She glared down at me before sticking her tongue out at me and stomping away.

"Old crazy bitch!" I mumbled as I finally found the strength to stand.

I had to rush the Uber driver through rush hour traffic to get to the probation office. My car was still impounded, and the police claimed they needed it for evidence in my case, so I had no choice but to let it sit. Kaila's old car spontaneously stopped cranking up, so I was forced to walk everywhere or use ride-share apps to get around. It would be my second meeting with my probation officer since I was released on bond after taking a plea deal. Apart from my release, there was an arrangement for me to check in every twenty-four hours, either by phone or in person; it was whatever my P.O. decided. Today, she wanted to see me in the office.

Before I walked inside, I dropped Keem a pin and asked him to scoop me once this was over. After watching me get my ass beat, he got in my ear about us working together to really take over. That nigga Kaila was fucking was very well connected, and lowkey, Keem was gunning for that nigga's head. Keem and I still needed to break bread and make a few plays to get to the paper.

"Yo' ass was this close to having this paperwork sent to the judge. Why are you late, Mr. Harris?" P.O. Stalls chastised me as soon as the bells on the office door chimed.

"I told you the other day I don't have transportation. It was traffic, and the Uber driver was going slow. I'm here now, though." Reaching into my pocket for my debit card, I was prepared to pay my probation fee when she pulled out a clear cup and set it on the counter.

"You've already paid up for the week. I need a urine sample."

"What am I supposed to do with the cup? I'm not thirsty." I scratched my head, looking around the office for a water fountain.

"You piss in it. I swear you niggas don't go to the doctor enough. It's a routine drug test. Would you prefer to go into the hospital so they can draw your blood?"

"Nah, I got it. I was just a little confused." I hadn't been to the doctor for a check-up since I was in grade school. That uptight bitch was talking to me like I was still riding the short bus every morning.

While I filled the cup, she stood over my shoulder to monitor me. I hadn't even touched a blunt yet since I had a feeling she would be on some bullshit before the week was out.

"As part of your terms, you will be allowed to leave your house for work or school, and if you have your children in your custody for over three hours. I am expecting you to secure legal employment within the next two weeks, or we'll have a different kind of conversation. Do I make myself clear?"

"Sir, yes, sir!" I saluted, and she scowled at me, causing me to laugh. "I'm sorry. I agree."

"Sign this, then you can be on your way. Your drug test came back clean. I expect it to be clean every time I test you." She slid the documents over to me along with a pen.

I quickly scribbled on each of them before making my exit.

"Nice ankle bracelet nigga!" Keem and I slapped hands as I walked out of the probation office. The music from his car was still blasting as the sun was setting for the evening.

"You know they couldn't keep a real nigga down."

"Already, man. Let's get the fuck out of here. This office is giving me flashbacks." Keem laughed as he walked off.

We got into his Camaro, and Alexia was sitting in the back seat with a smile on her face. This hoe knew I was still mad at her for how she did me in Orlando, but I wasn't going to address it in front of Keem. Truthfully, she played the game how it was supposed to be played. I was more than sure she got a larger cut than I did for her role in everything, so I had to respect her hustle.

She passed me a blunt to spark up and quickly took a long pull from it as Keem pulled out of the probation office's parking lot.

When I was allowed to make my first phone call in jail a few nights ago, I got Ann to make a three-way call to let Keem know what was happening. I was facing charges of DUI, disorderly conduct, reckless endangerment, and driving with a suspended license. The lawyer Ann found for me discussed all my charges, and I was surprised the state offered a deal. Keem looked out and posted the money for me to be released without thinking twice.

"What's the move been? I need to make a play ASAP. These lawyers ain't cheap, and my P.O. is talking about me finding something legit."

"Shit, I don't even know. Until we figure out what the hell Green has up his sleeve, we gotta lay low."

"That nigga popped up at my Aunt's house. He heard everything we talked about in the O, and he wants an even cut on everything we get," I revealed.

"Damn...I should've pulled the plug on his ass. Now we both gotta watch our backs," Keem grumbled.

"I did that shit because I thought it would take care of itself. I told Doc to keep the nigga alive, but I didn't mean to revive him completely. And I know that nigga Tyree is looking at me sideways about how I'm running shit. I wouldn't be surprised if he popped back up to boot me out of the way. Shit has been coming at me from every direction; I feel like I can't even breathe right."

"Man, speaking of that nigga, why the fuck you let him beat my ass like that? You spared Green, but you couldn't spare me? What the fuck was that about?"

"I don't know what you did to that man, but the ass whooping he gave you was personal, and I didn't any parts in that." Keem chuckled.

"That nigga fucking my BM, dawg. I don't know how long they've been creeping around. I can admit I was out here doing dirt, so I shouldn't be mad, but it's a hard pill to swallow, kid. I should've locked her ass down years ago, but I ain't ready for all that."

"Then you need to let her go. Tyree is a good nigga. His baby mamas are cool as fuck too."

"Man, fuck that fake ass Superman. Just because he's your people doesn't mean I approve of that shit. At the end of the day, she belongs to me. She got my jits, and we've been doing this shit for close to ten years. Kaila's ass ain't going nowhere. She's just mad right now. If I go buy her some shit, cry a little bit, and apologize, I'll have my girl back."

"That sounds good. You said she moved out, though, right?" Keem questioned, reminding me what I was going home to.

"She'll be back. Kaila's job doesn't pay that much, so I know she'll be begging me to move back in soon. I'll let her rock out for a month or two while I figure out how to get Ann out of my shit, then I'll have my family back."

"You putting money on that?" Keem challenged.

"Bet that up, nigga! A band, two bands... you let me know what your pockets can stand to lose."

"Ten bands says Tyree got her ass locked down. You better take your boys to get their suits and shit ready," he joshed. "I'll save you a seat next to mine at the wedding."

Keem was all teeth and laughing at my expense, but I still stood on the ten bands, and we shook hands. It wasn't another nigga out here that could take my woman or my kids from me. I put in too much time to let it go that easily.

Keem insisted on heading to the strip club, so we could eat and break bread, but I told the nigga I needed to stop by the house first to shower and get myself together. I was in the same clothes I got arrested in the other night, and I knew the bitches at the strip club would clown me if they saw me walk in wearing the same thing.

When we pulled up to my house, an old Buick was parked beside Ann's car in the driveway. "She probably got her fucking homegirls over here. One of them bitches drive that raggedy ass car all over this city. You coming in?" I asked Keem as I exited the car once he parked in front of the Buick.

He was right behind me as we headed inside. The front door was unlocked, and the scent of a home-cooked meal filled the air as we walked in.

"Damn, maybe I should leave. It smells like she threw down in here for you. I'll wait outside. She's probably in the room ass naked, waiting on you," he said before turning around to leave.

I laughed him off as I headed to the bedroom. "Ann! Whose car is that outside? Where are the kids? Why is it so quiet in here?" I yelled her name and asked rapid questions before opening the bedroom door.

Rose petals covered the floor leading to the bed, making me smile. A few candles illuminated the room, and I could see her silhouette on the bed. Light snores came from the bed, which caused me to halt my steps and turn on the light.

"Surprise, pussy nigga! Welcome home!" Green sat up in the bed and peeled the blankets back, revealing a naked Ann sprawled out. He smacked her on her bare ass while licking his lips. I could tell she was breathing, but she didn't move at the sound of our voices.

"Did you kill her, motherfucker?"

"Nah, after she whipped me up a hot meal, we had a few drinks, then I dicked her down. I see why you've been hitting this shit instead of Kaila. I'll give it an eight out of ten." He grinned. Green took his time getting out of bed as he grabbed his clothes off the floor to get dressed.

"You think you just gon walk out of here, nigga? You gotta see me about this shit," I raged, snatching the t-shirt he was trying to put over his head.

The wound on this throat was still healing, but he no

longer covered it with a bandage.

"I'm not seeing nothing about nothing. You tried to kill me, nigga! I could've knocked this bitch, and them jits in the other room, but I spared them. How the fuck you cross your own family, Charvo? We grew up together, but you had a bitch try to kill me. Nigga, you owe me!"

"I don't owe you shit. You're a snake-ass nigga who got what the fuck you deserved. If I wanted you dead, I would've done that shit myself. I'm not like you. I don't wait till mother-fuckers turn their heads to do them dirty; I'll look a nigga dead in his eyes and let him know what the fuck it is."

"Well, tell me what it is then, nigga, cuz, in my eyes, we ain't even family no more. I know you and that nigga Keem trying to run a play, and if you think that shit will be sweeter than what I've done for you, you're sadly mistaken, little cousin."

"Since we ain't family, keep this shit moving then. Don't let me catch yo' ass on this side of the city again. Auntie has a few black dresses hanging in the closet. It ain't nothing for her to throw one of them on for a Saturday morning service."

"Oh, you'll be seeing more of me from here on out. Pepperann and I talked, and it's time for me to be in my kids' lives. Appreciate you for stepping up to the plate, but their real daddy got it from here on out."

"The fuck you just say to me?" I was seeing red as I stared down the nigga who felt like the perfect stranger now.

"You heard me, nigga. That couch is pretty comfortable, so you can crash out there whenever I need to stay here to help with the kids."

"Fuck you, Gerald. Those kids came from my nutsack. I take care of my five. That's one thing I know I never have to worry about."

"I'm sure once the Molly wears off, she can explain to you

what's going on. I'm back in my city, nigga. You can choose to be with me or against me. But if you go against the grain, it ain't no saving you."

Green snatched his shirt from my hand and flinched at me, but I didn't move. I knew my revolver was on the nightstand beside the bed. Instead of giving this nigga another chance to one-up me, it was time for him to meet his maker.

I took two steps toward my nightstand and snatched the drawer open. As soon as the metal eased into my hand, Green rushed me and slammed my head into the open drawer.

"Fuck nigga, you want to kill me that bad? Do the shit right now, pussy!" Green raged.

My grip on the gun was firm as he tried to wrestle me for it. Although my body was almost back to normal from the Orlando beatdown, there were still places on me that were tender. Green tried to knee me in the groin, but I grabbed his leg, and we both tumbled to the ground. Wrestling over the gun, I felt my hand on it while his hand was on it. There was a brief moment of complete silence, then the loud gunshot echoed in my ears.

CHAPTER SIXTEEN

TYREE ROMAN

"How you let that little ass girl fuck up your motion, Tyree? This is how I know you've been off your game. Kaila is a great woman, and you just sat your stupid tail self up there and let that booty-scratching ass bitch run her off. I'm so disappointed in you." Starja was ripping into me as we sat in the restaurant for one of our monthly meetups. Vanessa sat beside her, silently shaking her head as she glanced over the menu.

"She walked outside looking for me, and Ashonte's crazy ass popped up. Y'all need to help me figure out how to get her back. Y'all over there judging me and shit. I ain't got time for it."

"You were supposed to be applying pressure as soon as the Orlando trip ended. It's no way you had her in the same suite, only separated by a thin ass wall, and you didn't leave with her number. You think he lost that magic touch?" Vanessa turned to Starja.

"I don't think he ever had it! I have never known Mr. Roman to be scared of a woman."

"I'm not scared—this situation is just different. There's a lot going on with her too. When we had a conversation, she told me she wanted to focus on herself and the kids right now. I did help her get everything situated with her apartment and took care of some legal stuff with her... I'm at a loss right now. I love both of you, but y'all ain't even have my head gone like this."

"Trust me, we know. We had a long conversation with her in Orlando. She'll make a good addition to our team, so you need to reach into that big ol' brain of yours and put something together. Kaila was great with all five of the kids. She had them fed and seated in that movie theater in less than thirty minutes. It would've taken Vanessa and I at least two hours to do that. She's very patient, nurturing, and loving. I love her for you, for all of us, because we already know if she's a part of you, we have to deal with her too."

"All of that sounds good, but I have to figure something out. Let's review the calendar, though. I have a meeting when this ends."

"With Jaxson?" Vanessa eyed me curiously.

"Touch your nose, baby mama. Back to the business."

As usual, we reviewed the calendar for the kids and started discussing plans for their summer break. Usually, Vanessa and TJ went up north to spend time with her family in New York, but since she and Jaxson were going steady, she expressed wanting to stay in Miami. He would be proposing to her in the coming months. I always remembered Jaxson as a standup guy raised by a good family, so it was only fitting that they took their relationship to the next level.

Starja, on the other hand, enjoyed the single life. She was dating a guy last year, but when he was ready to take things to the next level, she broke it off with him, claiming that he was moving too fast. I tried telling her that when a man knew what he wanted, he applied pressure, but she wasn't trying to hear that. Truthfully, Starja was always scared of commitment. Even when we were doing our thing back in the day, she never pressed me about making our situation more than it was. She was cool with us fucking then going about her business until she needed a tune-up.

I appreciated the dynamics of the relationships we all shared. A lot of other niggas didn't care for the mother of their children, but mine were an essential part of my life. Although I had my kids almost the same amount of time as them, the fact that they put their own lives at risk to bring my seeds into the world made me respect them so much more.

"It's one more thing I forgot to tell y'all about that incident." I braced myself because I knew one of them would try to knock my head off my shoulders with the news I was about to drop.

"She pregnant, ain't it?" Starja blurted out.

"Yeah, that's what she said." I sighed.

Starja got up and stomped out of the restaurant without saying another word to me. Vanessa picked up her wine and downed the rest of it. She had a way of communicating without speaking, and I knew she was just as disappointed as I was.

"We'll have the kids to you on Friday, Tyree. Take care of yourself." She gave a fake smile as she got up with her belongings and left.

I knew I had gotten myself into a fucked up situation.

When the waitress approached, I ordered two more Whiskey neats and paid the tab. It seemed as if the uncertainties of life were coming at me left and right these days. After Jaxson and I met at the restaurant, he hit my phone a few days later, requesting my presence at a round table meeting. I wasn't expecting it to move so fast, but knowing how the

Bosses operated, it was only a matter of time before we had to deal with Keem.

Remembering how the meetings used to run when I was in charge, I arrived an hour earlier than the set start time. Jaxson pulled up at the same time as me, so we headed in together.

"I think Maestro will be here. From the message exchange I read last night, he should have an army with him."

"I thought you said we had time, Jax."

"I thought we did, but your boy reached out to the Mexicans. You know rule number one in this game."

We couldn't fuck with the Mexicans. You could spin a globe and land on any other country, but the Colombians, who were the head of our operations on the East Coast, didn't play that shit. Once the line was crossed, caskets had to drop.

"I don't know what the fuck that nigga got going on, man. I've been trying to hit him up so we could have a sit down, but he's been forwarding my calls and leaving my messages on read. I already know how this shit is going to end, unfortunately."

"Yeah, man, let's get this over with. I hate to bring you back into the game under these circumstances, but you may be the only reason they don't shut shit down in Miami completely. They know you, your face is good, and you know how to run the business. If it comes down to it, we can do it together."

"I'm trying to stay out, Jaxson. I gave this shit ten years of my life and took four bullets in the process. I might not be as lucky this time around. I'm doing the family shit, running multiple businesses—the timing couldn't be worse."

"But is it ever perfect?"

"I get what you're saying, but I have to think on it. My

family is straight for years to come. It ain't shit else I need or want out here that I can't go get with what I have right now."

"I hear all of that, Tyree, but what we're talking about right now is bigger than us. Maestro will only see that your former operation is endangering his entire operation. They want a solution, not tomorrow or next week but today."

As anticipated, the meeting started twenty-seven minutes before the start time, so even if you were early, you were late.

"It's been a long time since I've been in Miami, and despite the circumstances, this is still one of my favorite cities. It's nice to see so many familiar faces, especially yours." Maestro pointed directly at me as all eyes fell on me. "That last time we talked, I remember you gift-wrapped your operation and handed it to your partner on a silver platter."

"I remember that," Maestro's right hand agreed with him as he raised a glass to me.

"So, how did we get here? What's his name? Keef, Krack... whatever the fuck the boy's name is. He knew the fucking rules and the bylaws, and now we have another fucking snake reaching out to the motherfucking Mexicans! Do they know who the fuck I am?" Maestro's voice boomed through the over-sized garage. With all the dramatics he could muster up, he paced the floor as if he were in deep thought. I knew this dog and pony show all too well. There were new faces at the round table, so he had to show them that he was all about standing on business.

"I need a solution, and I need it now," Maestro spoke just above a whisper.

His right-hand man approached the table with a red envelope and took the contents out one by one before spreading them across the table. Each page was a blown-up photo of everyone involved in the scheme that Keem and Green pulled off a few weeks ago.

"These two were the masterminds behind all of this. From what we've gathered, they brought in a third man, which is this clown." A picture of Kaila's baby daddy graced the table, which caused me to stand up from my seat. If they had his pictures, I knew they more than likely made the connection between him and Kaila. He then placed down a picture of the woman who was also in Orlando at Keem's place. I remembered seeing her at Keem's spot.

"We need these four faces, and Maestro wants them alive. We'll proceed with this if we can't get to them."

Pictures of their family members, including women, children, and elders, appeared as if the folder's contents were endless. Amongst the last few photos was a smiling Kaila in her license picture, followed by a single photo of each of her children. I assumed they were in the pickup line outside their school because they all wore uniform shirts in their photos.

My throat went dry as I felt like the air was being sucked out of the room. Knowing the innocence of Kaila and the kids had me ready to say fuck my retirement. I didn't owe her shit, but I knew I felt for her, and I wasn't going to let shit happen to her if I was the one who could stop it. Maestro didn't give a fuck who had to go when it came to people crossing him. With my own eyes, I had witnessed him blow up a house full of family on a Christmas morning almost twenty years ago. And when he did that, he was only sending a warning. His ass was much older and crazier now; it was no telling what he would do.

"I have your solution," I exclaimed before fully processing my decision.

"And what's that?" Maestro stopped pacing and stared at me.

"I'm back. I'll handle them."

CHAPTER SEVENTEEN

KAILA MOFFETT

Reading over my college acceptance letter to Broward College made me grin as I sat in the pedicure chair. As Tyree instructed and based on the terms listed in my lease agreement, I signed up for the associate of arts program since I had a few credits to go to earn my first degree. I was still undecided on what I wanted to study after that, but I needed to get it started.

"Is this color okay?"

Looking down at my toes, I checked the nail technician's polish and approved the sunflower yellow.

Since the kids had a three-day weekend coming up, I decided to take half a day off from work to have some me time before our busy weekend. I planned to take them out to a water park and a trampoline park since we hadn't done anything fun since our Orlando trip.

"Is that her sitting over there?" I heard a woman talking but didn't pay her any mind since I figured she wasn't talking about me.

"Kaila, is that you over there?" I looked in her direction,

and Vanessa stood with three different bottles of nail polish in her hand.

"Hey, girl! How are you?" Vanessa walked over to me and gave me a side hug before kissing my cheek.

"I'm good. Do you come here often?" I inquired. This was my second time at this salon, and I only came here because it was the closest to my job.

"I do. This is my spot. It's never busy, and they do amazing work."

"Well, I'm happy I picked this place. I work down the street at the nonprofit, so I stopped here before getting the kids. It's so good to see you. I hope the kids and Starja are doing well too."

"I'm on the phone with her right now. She said what's up."

I smiled, thinking about Starja's outgoing personality. She was the life of the party during the Orlando trip, even though it was last minute for them. I thought she would be the one to give me a hard time about being in Tyree's suite when we didn't even know each other, but she made the experience much more enjoyable.

I zoned out and got back into my phone as I finished reading over the next steps for me to start my classes. I needed to make time to meet with an academic advisor, order books, and get a few supplies to get started. I was already dreading the long days and nights that would come with doing my homework and helping the kids with theirs, but I kept telling myself that it would all be worth it in the end.

"You know we need to talk, right," Vanessa said as she sat in the pedicure chair beside me to get hers done.

"Girl, I tried, Vanessa. I know what we talked about, and I know you told me to have a little patience with him, but I've been through enough. All I did was walk outside to make sure he was okay, and another woman was sitting on his damn truck, talking out the side of her neck about me, and he stood there looking stupid. Didn't say anything to defend me. You don't even know how much that hurt my feelings."

"Knowing Tyree, he had to address her when you weren't in his presence. There is a side to him that can be almost impossible to digest. You might look at him differently if you see him in that light."

"Hell, I would've liked to see or hear something. I was ready to put everything I said aside and see where it would go with him. The kids were attached to him when they walked into that suite in Orlando. He literally had us on the best vacation we've ever been on. I didn't have to tell them no to anything the entire weekend because I didn't have the money or the time. I used to find myself working while on vacation just to make extra money to pay the bills once we got back in town. Tyree literally showed me a completely different side of life, but I feel like that was just a damn fairy tale. I know I have a lot going on, but he does, too. I want him to work out whatever he has going on, then maybe we can revisit this, say, this time next year?" I shrugged.

"That long, Kaila? Come on, now. I'm telling you, he's a great man. We need you as our third party; you fit perfectly into Starja and I's puzzle. The kids got along great. Give it a few weeks so you both can come back with clear heads and a new plan."

"I hear you, but it's not on me this time. I laid my intentions out for him already. If he wants me, he'll do what he has to do to get right. If not, then it's just not meant to be. I can accept that. We'd make great friends at the end of the day."

"Pshhh, I'm not hearing that." Vanessa waved me off.

"In other news, I'll be starting school this summer. I still have to figure out what I want to study for my bachelor's, but at least I can finally finish what I started. I'll be loading up my coursework to get the rest of my credits by the end of December, and then I will start the next program in January."

"Congratulations! We should go out tonight and celebrate. I remember you talking about wanting to go back. I'm happy for you, boo."

"Thank you! But I can't hang out tonight. The kids will be home for the next three days, and our party starts tonight." I giggled.

"You should bring them by the house. We can have some mommy time with a nice bottle of wine while the kids have fun. I'm sure Starja can meet up with us, too."

"I like the sound of that. It's been a while since I had a real mom's night." I smiled.

Vanessa and I talked a little more while we got our pedicures. I enjoyed being able to have a real conversation with her and getting to know more about her. She worked at a high school as a Guidance Counselor, and she was more than content with her job. I admired the way she carried herself and how highly she spoke of herself. She didn't do it in a way that said she was cocky; it was more like she knew she worked her ass off to get where she was in life, and there was nothing wrong with her wanting to celebrate that.

Almost an hour later, I was rushing out of the nail salon to make it to the kids' pickup line. I wasn't running late, but I knew they'd complain if I had them out there waiting too long in this heat.

The smooth traffic had me on the other side of the city in a matter of minutes. As I maneuvered through the neighborhood, my mind was on Tyree. I was fighting the urge to pick up my phone and text him, especially after my conversation with Vanessa. I told myself that I needed to stand on business regarding my feelings and heart. I refused to have another man out here doing me any way and getting away with it. If he wanted me, he'd be the one to come back with an over-the-top apology and straight pressure.

"Hey, my babies," I greeted the kids as they got into the car.

As usual, they all tried to talk to me at the same time to fill me in on their day. I loved that my children loved school, and they each excelled academically. Every quarter, we received invitations to the honor roll ceremonies that highlighted the kids. I was a damn proud mother, and I knew this shit was really just beginning. There was so much more I wanted for my babies, and I was ready to do whatever it took to make it happen.

"Do y'all want to stop for ice cream?" I asked, noticing a Baskin Robbins down the road.

"Yes! Let's get this party started." Cadell was dancing in his seat.

"Listen, do y'all remember the kids y'all met when we stayed at the nice hotel in Orlando?"

"You mean Shaniyah and TJ?" Taika asked.

"It's Shariyah, baby, but yes, them. Their mom invited us over tonight. How would y'all feel about that? We can order pizza while y'all play, watch movies, and get in the pool." I said, trying to sweet-talk them into going even though I knew it wouldn't take much.

"That sounds good to me. I liked playing with Shariyah. She doesn't have a sister, and neither do I, so we had a lot of fun."

Smiling inwardly at my daughter's response, I knew we'd be over there tonight having a grand ol' time.

"What's up with you, Kambrel? You've been quiet, baby."

"I'm cool, Mom. If I can bring the Playstation, I'm down." He shrugged. My son was too damn cool for me. He was a chill baby coming up, and now he was evolving into a nonchalant tween. He was all in as long as he had good food, his game system, and sports.

Taika and I sang along with the song playing on the radio as I pulled into the Baskin Robbins parking lot. I hated going through the drive-thru at that location because once you got in the line, you couldn't get out until you received your order. Going against my better judgment, I still pulled up behind the last car in the line and waited our turn to place our order at the speaker.

I was searching through my purse when a car pulled up behind us, slamming into the back of my Suburban. They had to be going at least fifty miles an hour in the parking lot.

"Are y'all okay?" I asked the kids.

Cadell was crying while Kambrel and Taika were trying to figure out what was happening. Before I knew it, three masked people had surrounded my truck with guns fixed on us.

"If you make any sudden moves, I'll shoot your fucking face off, bitch! Open your door slowly."

Looking ahead, the car in front of me was gone. I thought about slamming on the gas and getting the fuck away from those people, but I had to think twice. I was sure the bullets in their guns could travel way faster than my truck.

"My kids are in here with me… please don't hurt my kids." I expected other onlookers to come to my aid in broad daylight, but it seemed to be a ghost town.

A single gunshot went through my front windshield. "Next time, that'll be in your fat-ass skull, bitch. Open your fucking door."

"Mommy—" Takia's voice trembled as she pleaded for me to keep them safe.

"We just have to listen to these people, baby. We won't get —" Taika's door was opened, and right before my eyes, my daughter was snatched out of the truck.

I fumbled to get my seatbelt off and get out of my truck. By the time my feet hit the pavement, their cars were reversing out of the parking lot, narrowly missing the large dumpsters.

"Taika!!!" I screamed my daughter's name as I ran across the grass, trying to catch the car.

As I fell to my knees, the car slipped into traffic, and eventually, the car's taillights disappeared.

To be continued...

Made in the USA
Las Vegas, NV
18 July 2024

92553261R00111